I0607683

THE LOLLIPOP MAN

Kevin Sweeney

Black Rainbows Press

ISBN 978-1-8384613-0-0

Black Rainbows Press
www.blackrainbowspress.com

For Pinky

Coming soon from the same author...

THE SHOPPING LIST
THE GARDEN GNOME
THE CROP CIRCLE
THE MICROWAVE

And, exclusively at GODLESS.COM...

THE LUSTY
THE GLUTTONS
THE SLOTH
THE GREEDY & THE ENVIOUS
THE WRATHFUL
THE PROUD

ONE

"*PEEEEEEE-DOOOOOOO...*"

Every morning it was the same ritual. Half a dozen voices calling out the same two syllables across the road Bartleby had his back to.

"*Peeeeee-dooooo...*"

They waited somewhere just out of sight, around the corner, until all the others kids were across and on school grounds. It was only after every other kid, on foot, on bikes, on push scooters and the parents, many dressed for the day jobs they would rush to afterwards, the odd eccentric in their pyjamas, and the dogs that the parents brought along for the early morning walk... not until the rush was over would the Skeleton gang appear.

"*Peeeeee-dooooo...*"

When it had started at the beginning of the year, there had been times when some parents were around when they had started to call to him. A few of those parents had tried to intervene. But no mum or dad tried more than once, and now they were never to be seen when the ritual began. As for any teachers... they apparently knew better, because even when he had raised the issue with the school, nothing had been done. If the issue wasn't on the school grounds, they did not want to know.

"*Peeeee-dooooo...*"

Cars were infrequent now the worst of the morning rush was over, but he still had a duty of care.

Bartleby stood up as straight as he could and turned around.

She was looking straight at him, as she always did. The next part of the ritual would be signalled by her saying the word alone, shaping the syllables carefully so that he could read them on her thin lips.

"*Peedo.*"

He shuddered inside his hi-vis trench coat, and even though he was sure it wasn't visible because the stiff, fluorescent material was more like a sheath hanging from his shoulders than clothes proper, she still grinned.

He held his sign up, even though no vehicles were approaching from either direction, and he walked out into the road. When he was halfway across he stopped and made a barrier of himself, his pole braced against the tarmac just to one side of the white road marking of a stick figure flanked by two smaller figures. Then he looked at the half a dozen children who waited patiently for his signal. Five of them were at least a head taller than their leader, but it was to her that your gaze was always drawn.

Her surname was Skelton, which meant the other children might have naturally started calling her Skeleton even if she hadn't be so painfully skinny. But not only was she thin, she was short as well. It was hard to think that in a modern country like the UK childhood malnutrition still existed, but stood there on the curb staring at him was the proof. Her black hair was thin, her clothes a shabby second hand uniform sizes too big for her, which only made her seem tinier, frailer, except for her eyes. Her eyes were far older than her eleven years of life, and full of cruel laughter. Her gaze took in a person as if they could see the soul itself, and found something darkly amusing in what they saw.

Bartleby beckoned the children to cross.

Skelton stepped down onto the tarmac first, the others always a step behind. Her shoes were scuffed, the laces of the left one broken and knotted back together, but she walked as if she owned the road, as if, perhaps, she owned even Bartleby himself.

The twins followed, the boys flanking her like bodyguards. Then, behind them in a loose row, the tubby girl, the tall girl, and the ugly boy.

He knew it was wrong to simply label them this way, and he knew each of their names and nicknames, but he could not help himself. In the Skelton girl's presence they seemed to be reduced, even if each of them wore newer and cleaner clothes than her, looked healthier, better fed, looked more like the children they actually were... her shadow fell on them each.

In the early weeks of the ritual, when the occasional parent had attempted to correct them as a group or the Skelton girl singly on Bartleby's behalf, the other children had each attempted to stifle their giggling at their leader's shocking behaviour. But somehow, gradually, their glee at their vicarious naughtiness had changed; it took him some time to realise that they were no longer enjoying their ability to attack an authority figure, but continued because the Skelton girl wanted to.

Just as she passed him, almost as an afterthought, she said, "I know you're thinking about sticking your cock in my pussy, you dirty old cunt."

It was only after she said it, walking by, that she would then look back at him, and wink.

And then the Skeleton Gang -a name that should have been cute- reached the other side of the road safely and made their way to school just before the teacher in the playground rang the bell.

*****

He'd been in the job nearly four years and he believed that he had gotten used to the evil little shits. In his experience there was a new batch of them every year, as the oldest year group reached the threshold of adolescence a few of the apple cheeked cherubs turned rotten. He was an authority figure, but his authority was limited, and they knew he had no ability to punish them, so each year there were always a few who began to push at the boundaries, and he was the perfect target.

Twat.

Wanker.

Sad bastard.

Yellow prick.

Bartleby had heard them all, and had reconciled himself to the fact that none of it was personal, just emerging personalities seeking to start defining themselves by opposition to a world that, until then, they had said "yes please" and "no thank you" in without question.

He believed that he was immune to it. The other children, the younger ones who drew him pictures, who insisted on holding his hand as they crossed, chatting about the latest fads that made up the whole of their internal landscapes and who gave him boxes of chocolates at the end of the school year, they made the job worthwhile.

But... but there was something different about the Skelton girl.

Her eyes. Her dead, laughing eyes.

Peee-dooo.

He dreamed about her, at first only once a month, but as time went on, more and more.

Peee-dooo.

Weeks of the same routine, the only variation the obscenity she muttered to him as she crossed. But always the same chorus came first.

"*Pee-do.*"

Bartleby started. The memory of the voice was so clear that he swore that he heard it, right next to his ear... but of course he hadn't. Not really. He lived alone, had done since his mum had passed.

He was sat on the edge of his bed. He didn't know how long he had been there. His uniform hung inside the wardrobe. The door was open. He'd sat down to pull his socks off, and then he had seen the long bright yellow coat hanging there and it had set him thinking, daydreaming.

Pee-do.

Paedophile. No child had ever called him that before. They swore at him, those rotten apples who next year would find themselves in secondary school, suddenly at the bottom of the social totem pole again, but none had ever used that word.

He leaned forward and closed the wardrobe door. His room was only small, the house too. He could have moved somewhere much bigger, but he did not want the extra space. He liked his childhood home, liked the way it made him feel connected to a time long gone. This was the house in which his mother had raised him, before passing away last year, leaving him without direction. But when he closed the door, the mirror that hung on the outside came into view and he saw himself, and he was no child anymore.

Bartleby suddenly saw himself as the girl saw him. A sad man, a sagging man, a man who helped children cross the road just so that he could be close to them... And why would any grown man want to be close to children that were not his own?

It was an epiphany that seemed to crawl through him, a prickling light that moved steadily through the dark coils of his brain to illuminate each moist shadow.

He had told himself that she had not got under his skin, but she had. She had.

He saw himself as something to be despised. Loathed.

"I know you're thinking about sticking your cock in my pussy, you dirty old cunt."

And Bartleby decided he could no longer live this way.

*****

The children talked about what had happened to the lollipop man. Of course they did. They asked their parents, their teachers, but the answers were never satisfactory. They just said he had gone away, and there would be a new lollipop person coming soon. And there was, a nice lady called Mrs Pankhurst, and soon one year of children grew up and moved onto their next school, and then another, and another, and by the time ten years had passed no-one remembered Mr Bartleby... except as a story told amongst children who had never met him... that there was once a lollipop man who killed himself by walking out into the path of a lorry without his lollipop pole, and that his ghost now haunted the road where he had worked and died.

Ten years passed…

TWO

WHEN SHE opened it she expected a cock, but instead found a mystery.

Krissi Skelton had just settled down at the kitchen table to do some paperwork when her phone had vibrated with a notification.

Her natural reaction to unsolicited communication on Facebook was to assume it was unwanted male attention. Nine times out of ten, it was, mostly pics of bloke's genitals, either flaccid or aroused. She didn't know which was funnier, the mugshots of anteater cocks with drippy noses, or bright red, angry looking erections that always made her think of Mr Punch.

Anteater or Punch... I'm guessing... Punch!

But not this time.

Nine times out of ten... well, this was one of those tenth times...

She hadn't even been going to open it, except that she had taken on some new ladies recently, and it could have been one of them. Most of her clients were middle aged or older, and they weren't always great with tech. There was a chance it was a newer client trying to make a booking, or had passed along her details to a friend who was trying to make an appointment.

The message was not a dick pic. It was a birthday cake.

It was a child's cake, the kind you picked up in ASDA at the last minute, even though you promised yourself that you were going to be Supermum and make one yourself this year, but there were only so many hours in every day... It was in the shape of a hedgehog, with chocolate fingers for spines, and a smiley animal face made out of dolly mixture sweets. There were two candles stabbed into its head, rainbow coloured ones, a pair of numbers, a figure two and a figure one.

Twenty-one.

The candles weren't lit. It wasn't the kind of cake you had for somebody turning twenty-one. Twenty-one used to be the age you became an adult, only nowadays that meant it was basically a chance to re-run your eighteenth. But it definitely didn't involve a cheap kiddie cake from the shops.

Bit weird...

She tapped on the sender's details.

The name was SCRIVENER. The profile pic was a slightly blurry image of two black sticks fingers, one slightly larger than the other, both walking, on a bright yellow background.

She frowned. It looked familiar, but for the life of her she couldn't place where she had seen something like it before.

There was another pic in the message thread, further down.

What the frig...

More hedgehog birthday cakes, six in total, in a line on a floor of black and white checked tiles.Well, she assumed the destroyed brown masses on the left had been hedgehog cakes, judging by the dolly mixture sweets and broken candles visible in the mess, cakes that had been smashed flat with something, or stamped on by a huge boot, turning them into exploded brown masses of dough and cream and raspberry jam.

The dark red, thick jam filling made them look disturbingly like real hedgehogs that had been run over, blood and guts squirting from ruptured flesh.

The remaining cakes were all the same as the first pic, each sporting a pair of candles, a number two and a number one.

She shuddered.

The two pictures had no explanation to them. Was this a joke? If it was, she couldn't see what the point was. It was just utterly bizarre. And warped; who would buy a load of cakes, and then destroy two of them? It was a waste of food. Also, stupid as it was, she felt a bit sorry for the cakes; she had two dolls on her bed, and she felt bad if she woke in the morning to find one lying on the floor, knocked off in the night by her tossing and turning. She knew they were just dolls, but didn't like the idea of one being cold and lonely all night... and in the same silly way, she felt sorry for the poor hedgehog cakes being so brutally destroyed...

It's a threat.

Once the thought was there in her mind, it stood stark and lucid and it felt utterly right. A threat? Yes, that was it, she was sure, positive. Whoever this Scrivener bloke was -and it had to be a bloke, that she was sure of, too- he had sent her a surreal and sinister message, a warning, a promise.

But why?

Her phone vibrated and she almost dropped it, for just a split second sure that it was a call, that it would be the sender of the pictures somehow psychically picking up on her question and eager to tell her the awful answer. But it wasn't. It was just the reminder to pick up her son from school, an alarm she set whenever she found herself sitting down to concentrate on her business paperwork... paperwork which had been ignored owing to the unpleasant mystery of the half dozen birthday cakes.

*****

Sam was quiet on the walk home, but Sam was always quiet. He tended to answer questions with shakes of his head, nods, and shrugging his shoulders.

"Did you have a nice day at school?"

A slow, thoughtful nod.

Krissi walked with her arms folded. Sam had his hands in his pockets, his Paw Patrol backpack bobbing as he watched his feet, careful to never step on the edges of the paving stones. She had to fold her arms to stop herself from touching him, to place a hand around one painfully thin shoulder; because he hated to be touched in public.

"Did you have maths today?"

A quick shake, left right left.

"English?"

A nod.

"Did you read for Miss Brite?"

A shrug of the shoulders; he had done, but he hadn't wanted to. She knew his reading was getting better though. She'd heard him, in his room with the door open a crack, reading *Alice's Adventures in Wonderland* one word at a time but getting faster in how he sounded out the difficult ones.

"Did you have art today?"

She already knew the answer, but wanted his reaction.

He actually looked up at her, briefly, and grinned as he nodded, before going back to watching where he trod.

"So you have some pictures for me?"

A half shrug, but seeing as though this was art he actually explained himself.

"It's not finished."

"Ah," she said. "So I can't see it yet?"

A nod.

"Not even a peek?"

A shake.

"It's cauliflower cheese tonight. Sound good?"

A nod.

"If you like we can stop in the newsagents on the way and you can get a can of fizz."

"Dandelion and burdock," he said.

"It speaks! Twice in one day, will wonders never cease, and yuck, what is wrong with your taste-buds? Last time it was that bubblegum flavoured stuff..." Her phone rang. She read the screen. Bugger."'"Scuse me, puppy, I have to answer this."

A shrug.

It was Mrs Neuberg, and of course, it was an emergency. She had decided to have another go at dying her hair herself, and yet again, there clearly had to have been something wrong with the instructions because now... Krissi listened until she saw an opening to slide a word in, and quickly assured the daft old bag that she would be around right away to work a minor miracle.

When she ended the call she stopped walking. Sam halted in the exact centre of a paving slab.

"Sorry puppy, we have to go and save one of my ladies from themselves. It'll only be an hour or so."

Sam shrugged.

"And then we'll get that nasty can of fizz. Hmm, cauliflower cheese washed down with dandelion and burdock, yum."

*****

It was simplest to go round and see exactly what the damage was first, rather than head home and get her supplies, as it was only a short detour to Mrs Neuberg's place... though it was amazing what only a few streets difference made as far as property. Krissi and Sam lived in the bottom flat of a converted terrace house, but just two left turns and a right, and straight over the crossroads, brought you to the large semi-detached places where a good number of her clients lived.

Her hunch was right; Mrs Neuberg's hair might have turned a shade of green suggesting she had been swimming in a pool with too much chlorine, but it was nothing that couldn't be sorted with a second box of the dye she had used.

Krissi bit her tongue about the fact that a regular client like Mrs Neuberg had been trying to sort her dye job out on her own, obviously to save a few quid... It would have been nice to tell the woman to get stuffed, that she deserved it for being both a skinflint and too stupid to follow simple instructions, but when you got down to it, she couldn't afford to lose anyone from her books.

And besides, when one of her ladies did something stupid like this, it just reinforced the fact that they needed her.

Mrs Neuberg hadn't been happy that Sam was in tow, but even that worked to Krissi's advantage.

"Well, you did say it was an emergency," she explained. "We were walking home from school when you called, and I thought it best to whip around here right away."

"Well, yes, I suppose that makes sense," said Mrs Neuberg with a sniff.

Reluctantly, she offered the boy a seat at the kitchen table, a glass of heavily diluted blackcurrant squash, and a plate with a single biscuit.

"Sam, puppy, you just stay here while Mrs Neuberg and I go upstairs to the bathroom and sort out those nitwits at Schwartzkopf, okay?"

He didn't look thrilled at the prospect.

Well, there was always every 21st century parent's ace up the sleeve.

"Here's my phone," she said, handing it over. "Stay under my data allowance, this won't take long."

*****

It wasn't until later, after fixing Mrs Neuberg's dye job and getting home to a dinner of cauliflower cheese washed down with cream soda - the newsagents had stopped stocking dandelion & burdock- that she discovered something odd.

The messages from the Scrivener, along with the pics of the hedgehog cakes, were gone.

Sam was in his room, drawing.

She knocked on the door, even though it was always ajar.

"Puppy, I've got a question for you," she said, standing in the doorway.

He looked up from his drawing, curling one protective arm around the picture so that she couldn't make it out. Whatever it was, he had used a lot of yellow to colour it.

"When I gave you my phone earlier, did you delete anything on it?"

He nodded.

"Was it something on my social media?"

He nodded again.

"You know you shouldn't have done that, Sam," she said. "It could have been one of my clients, or something else that was important."

He just looked at her.

"Why did you do it Sam?"

He blinked, and then, as if explaining something very simple to someone who should have already known, he answered;

"He's a bad man. He's supposed to be good, but he's not. He's bad."

Then he bent back to his drawing.

THREE

NADIA WALSH didn't think of herself as innocent, or sexually naive, but when Duane had first told him what he wanted for his birthday she had thought he was talking about food. A "spit-roast" was where they cooked a whole pig, yeah? She'd seen one at a school fete once, turning and turning, the cook carving off chunks of moist flesh and crispy crackling into a floured bap, and even though the meat was juicy enough to eat on its own, there were mucky bottles of brown sauce and sweet chilli and ketchup on a plastic patio table next to...

Nadia shook her head of the memory or daydream. Being wishy-washy, she hated that. "Always woolgathering, you are, girl," her mam would say. It was a bit scary, zoning out so completely. Like now; she was already standing in front of the buttons for the flats, and she couldn't remember the walk from the car park. Scary, because it was dangerous; she was wearing a dress so tight that you could, as her mam would have put it, "see what you'd had for breakfast." That and thigh high boots, which Duane had requested she wear as an "extra" to his actual birthday present, meant she really should be fully alert, even in a nice bit of town like this.

She asked herself again whether this was a good idea.

She probably should have seen this coming at some point.

The twins shared everything else, after all.

Still, it was her choice, and she had said yes. It was a reluctant yes, a yes which had bits attached to it -that this was only going to happen once, and no, you can't take pictures or film it, no, nope, not happening- but she had agreed and Nadia was as good as her word because she prided herself on settling her mind on stuff and not being wishy-washy. So not only was she going to do this, she was going to give it her all.

Anyway, YOLO, yeah?

She pressed the button. The intercom buzzed. Eventually, Duane answered.

"That you, babe?"

Nadia rolled her eyes. There was a camera. She hated redundancies like that. Wishy-washy.

Still, you only turned twenty one once...

She shoved the tip of her nose upwards with one finger and looked up into the lens.

"Oink, oink!" she said.

*****

It wasn't Duane who opened the door for her, but somebody with his face.

"Good evening, Nadia," said Cliff. "I trust you are well?" He was always oddly formal. If Nadia hadn't known he was mildly autistic, and that it wasn't an an affectation so much as a compulsion, she would have told him to stop it because it made him sound like a prick.

"Hi Cliff," she said.

His eyes were already running down her body, making every inch of her skin aware of how the material of her dress was hugging her.

Oddly formal, but still creepy. He spoke like a gentleman, but his actions betrayed him.

If I didn't love your brother...

"You going to let me in?" she asked.

He stepped back and to the side, one hand extended like a waiter gesturing to a table.

"Please," he said, smiling.

As she walked passed she felt how round her bum was, packed and lifted in her dress. She felt his eyes on the curves of her buttocks as they rolled up and down.

It was a short corridor that lead to the living room, which was open plan with the kitchen. Duane was stood at the breakfast bar, opening a bottle of wine and pouring a tall glass for her.

Duane's face was flushed. He was excited.

"You wore the boots," he said, and his voice was a little thick.

She took the glass from him, and drained it before handing it straight back for a top up.

"You know I hate redundant..." She stopped herself. "Yes, yes I did! The birthday boy gets what he wants!"

But before that, she'd need the rest of the bottle inside her.

*****

They had met at a function that head office had put on for the area sales managers, a day out at the rugby, to watch the county team that the firm sponsored, with a slap up feed afterwards and a meet and greet with the players. Nadia had been brought along in her official capacity as junior personal relations officer, though the truth was she was there as “totty”.

The sales director’s own word.

Should I call human resources? Let me think, hmmm, cushy job with a fat salary and all I have to do is make sure I’m never alone in a room with the slimy fuck... no brainer.

She’d seen Duane perform on the pitch and noticed even at a distance that he was a rather nice looking “lump of a fella,” as her mam said when she’d sent her the first selfie of them together (relationship milestone!) At the meet and greet she’d made a point of seeking him out, and he looked so adorable in a suit that didn’t fit him, as awkward as a schoolboy, that she’d wasted no time in getting to know him. Twice.In the disabled toilet.

It was on their second proper date that he told her about his twin, awkward, autistic Cliff, who he looked after.

At first, Nadia found this endearing...

*****

Two bottles after arriving she was lying on her stomach over the oat coloured footrest in the middle of the living room, naked except for her boots as the brothers prepared to flip a coin for who took which end.

Her knees were on the ground and her arms were crossed, propping herself up on her elbows. Her pussy was shaved, her lips slightly parted in a sticky pucker. She'd slavered herself in cactus blossom scented lubricant, and was wondering if this would take long as the wine had sharpened the edge on her hunger. She'd missed lunch.

"Can we get a pizza after?" she asked. "Something spicy. I need something spicy."

Duane and Cliff were stood in front of her, naked and nearly identical. Duane was much more muscular because of rugby, but otherwise they were identical except for their haircuts and the fact that Cliff was already erect. Long, very thick, veiny, with a drop of pre-cum sitting in the slit of his glans like an unshed tear.

"Pizza?" said Duane. "Yeah, sure, yeah, sounds good. Right, heads or tails?"

"She is your female companion, you should get to choose," said Cliff. "Also, your hands are shaking. Maybe I should flip the coin?"

"I'm just excited," said Duane, and laughed. "I can't believe we're going to do this! We always talked about it, but we never... shit, okay, here, you flip and I'll call."

Cliff took the coin, sent it spinning into the air with a flick of his thumb, caught it, and slapped it down on the back of his hand.

"So, exactly how long have you been talking about this?" asked Nadia, the alcohol slowing her reasoning so that now, belatedly, she sensed that maybe she had a reason to be a bit pissed off.

"Call."

"I dunno, really, probably since we..." said Cliff, before he looked at her and saw her watching him carefully. "Not about you, babe, just a spit-roast in general! We've talked about it since..." He stopped himself. "Oh shit, is there any answer which would be a good answer?"

"Please call," said Cliff.

Nadia sighed. He looked so crestfallen.

"Never mind, I'm a girl of my word..."

Duane grinned.

"Heads!" he said.

Cliff lifted his hand.

"Heads it is," he said. "Which means I will take the tail end."

Nadia found she was relieved. She was glad; yes, this way, the only face she would see was Duane's, looking down at her.

When Cliff turned, the drop of pre-cum shivered free and rolled down the length of his shaft.

She pointed a thumb at the bottle of cactus blossom lubricant on the glass coffee table.

"Grease that thing up," she told him. "Don't be stingy with the lube."

Cliff inclined his head, picked up the bottle and walked up closer to her, so close that his huge erection was only a foot from her face.

"Whatever you request," he said.

The bottle made a plastic, squelchy fart as he upended it and squirted the gel along the top of his shaft like coating a hot dog in ketchup.

Or brown sauce, or sweet chilli...

Woolgathering.

He was generous. Excess flowed around the thickness of him and began to drip onto the carpet.

Cock wagging in front, dripping sweet smelling goo, Cliff walked around to her rear.

"How about me babe, you want me to put some on?" asked Duane.

She smacked her tongue against the roof of her mouth. The wine had given her dry mouth.

"Be a good idea," she said.

He squirted a long stream of lubricant into his palm and began to massage himself, and as he worked his inches they plumped, flushed a deeper colour than the skin of his thighs, and twitched upwards into a rock hard horn.

Nadia moaned, a low sound deep in the back of her throat born of unconscious and unrestrained yearning. A huge cock on a thick, muscular body pressed her buttons.

She didn't tell him what to do, just reached for him, gripped him around the root, and pulled his cock towards her mouth. At the moment her lips engulfed the glistening plum of his glans, something equally as big and round pushed against her pussy.... then sank into her, filling her. Hands settled onto her hips, and a second pair gently cupped the back of her hand.

"Oh babe..." said Duane.

He filled her mouth, tongue pressed flat, as two, three, four inches of thick, slick cock pushed in. Simultaneously, something just as hot and huge crammed into her cunt.

Five, six, seven... eight...

To Nadia's surprise, the sensation was incredible. She was *taking* two men, not *being* taken. She was not being used, but asserting her own sexuality. She gripped the man she loved and pulled more of him into her mouth at the same time as she pushed back onto his brother, until both her soft palate and her cervix were being pressed by their organs.

She felt strong, powerful, sexy.

Duane groaned, and his twin gasped, his hands slipping down and grasping her buttocks as Duane's fingers wrapped themselves into her hair.

The intercom buzzed. It buzzed long and loud, as if the visitor below was impatient and knew that the flats occupants were busy, but did not give a shit.

"Oh what the fuck?" said Duane. "Sod off, we've only just got started!" he shouted, as if the intruder could hear.

Nadia let half of him glide over her lips before sucking it in again, signalling how she felt.

But Cliff had stopped pumping.

"We have a visitor, Duane," he said.

"Yeah I know, Cliff," said Duane, and Nadia knew why he sounded a little edgy; Cliff's need to be so formal. It was his autism, his way of dealing with the world. The problem was, even though strict manners allowed him to deal with what he otherwise found chaotic social interactions, it had become obsessive. He could not switch it off. "Never mind, mate, it's probably just a Just Eat or Deliveroo bloke who's hit the wrong button."

As if they'd heard this and wished to make it clear that it was not true, the person downstairs leaned on the intercom again, longer than before.

Nadia felt the solid erection in her pussy losing its thickness.

For the love of...

"They're rung twice now," said Cliff. "That wouldn't be a mistake. We can't leave them waiting."

"Cliff, no!"

It was no good. Cliff's rapidly deflating cock slid out of Nadia as the twin pulled away to go to the door and answer the summons.

"It would be the height of rudeness to let them ring thrice," he said as he went.

"Fuck!" said Duane.

Nadia pulled away from him, but kept her mouth tight so that there was a wet little pop as the tip of his cock left her mouth.

"Never mind, babe," she said. She gave his still firm shaft a long, slow squeeze along its length. "Here, let me just sort you out, just a nice blowy to finish you off..."

Out in the hallway, Cliff was speaking into the intercom, but whatever he was saying was indistinct with the distance.

Nadia kept sucking long and slowly on Duane's cock.

But Duane was shaking his head.

"No, this wasn't what we planned! Your twenty-first is special, and me and Cliff had always..." he looked down at her. "Babe, please, just stay there, yeah? I'll go get Cliff back, this won't take a moment."

Nadia sighed around his erection, then pulled her mouth off it.

"Fine. But hurry up, my knees are starting to ache."

Duane was already leaving the room.

Nadia sighed again, and slumped over the foot rest, head dangling down to stare at the carpet where Duane's heavy footprints were still clearly defined.

For fucks sake...

She loved Duane. She did. But every now and again she ran through scenarios in her mind about what the future might look like, deliberately woolgathering.

Moving in. Getting engaged. Marriage. Children, possibly. All the normal stuff of life.

And in every scenario, the issue of Cliff popped up and burst the daydream bubble. In every scenario, she saw herself making an ultimatum... and she saw herself losing.

Spit-roast. Her, them. Was it indicative of the shape of things to come?

She should have shot it down; and even though she prided herself on knowing her mind and never backing down, she was also not enough of a fool to deny that changing her mind was also her prerogative. She wasn't feeling sexy about it anymore; the fact that Duane had asked, and she had made a gift of herself, and then right in the middle of her making his fantasy come true he had left her to pursue his brother...

Fuck it.

She pushed herself up. Her dress was lying over the arm of the sofa. She scooped it up, headed towards the bathroom. She was going to clean herself up and then she was leaving. Nadia had just decided to force the issue, her thinking aided by a belly full of wine; Duane, time to make a decision, me or Cliff...

She closed the door behind her and started using fistfuls of toilet paper to clean up.

As she blotted a mixture of cactus blossom lubricant, pre-cum, and her own juices she felt her mood swing again, the weather-vane of her emotions turning towards weepy. But she wouldn't cry, she snarled in her mind. Not now. She'd given her heart and her body, but she'd be damned if Duane would have her tears...

Outside, in the flat, somebody shouted, a wordless cry muffled by the bathroom door and distance.

Then she heard Duane roaring, a sound similar to the cry of victory he made on the rugby pitch every time he scored a try... but the tone now was not of triumph.

There was a heavy thud, like something slammed against a wall.

Another.

The roar turned into a shriek.

Nadia felt frost growing down the length of her spine at the sound... and then, when the high pitch wail was suddenly cut off, an icicle flower with snowflake petals bloomed in her stomach.

From the first muffled cry to the suddenly silenced shriek must have been only a matter of ten seconds.

"Duane? What's going on?" she called. She crept closer to the door, straining to hear.

There was no answer.

"Duane?"

Had the twins had a fight? Perhaps Duane had become so frustrated at his brother that he had lashed out. She'd never seen him display anything more than resigned frustration with his brother's quirks before, but maybe with his blood up, adrenaline flowing and lust frustrated, a baser instinct had over taken him.

She never considered the possibility that Cliff had let the unwanted visitor in.

If she had, she may have acted differently.

Duane's dressing gown hung on the back of the door. She slipped it on. It smelled of Lynx Africa deodorant and the coal tar body scrub that he used.

"Duane? What's happened?"

She unlocked the bathroom door. The click of the lock was very loud.

"Duane? Please tell me what's going on! Are you two fighting?"

She pulled the door towards her slowly, cautiously, not because she was afraid of what may have been waiting for her, but because for all her bravado she hated conflict. If the twins were fighting she didn't want to see it, especially didn't want to see her boyfriend's sweet, open face twisted by anger.

Duane came staggering towards her like he was drunk, but he'd only had half a glass, and then she saw the reason he was staggering, heavy cock wagging between his muscular thighs, was because his head was chopped open, a huge gash splitting him from his crown to just above his left eyebrow, his skull yawning to expose his brain and making that side of his face slump as if he'd had a huge stroke. Blood under high pressure jetted in a stuttering fountain from the wound.

His right eye focused on her whilst the left darted back and forth.

"Bahhb?" he asked, one hand reaching towards her as he took two more steps before collapsing to his knees. "Waatahhpen?"

He slumped face first into the carpet, sending a bright arc of blood to whip down Nadia's face, blinding her and painting her lips.

She wiped her eyes by instinct, but they were still sticky with gore when she opened them to briefly glimpse something huge and bright darting towards her, and then pain exploded across the top of her head and she joined Duane on the floor.

*****

When she came to, she naturally assumed from the furry taste of stale wine in her mouth that her grogginess and the thumping in her skull were due to a hangover.

She sat up, slowly, aware of a delicate freight in her stomach which would have to be handled gingerly so that it didn't become vomit, red wine vomit, which would never come out of the bed-sheets.

But there were no sheets. She was on the sofa in Duane's flat.

This made no sense; if she ever spent the night it was never on the sofa. Why would she, when her big cushy boyfriend had a big cushy bed to curl up in, only steps away from the living room?

She was cold.

"Duane?" she croaked, trying to blink the sleep-crust out of her eyes.

Something was wrong.

The sleep crust was too thick, too sticky...

She remembered sucking Duane's cock. Her bruised brain put two and two together, and came up with seven; Duane had pulled out and spunked all over her face, and then she'd fallen asleep with his come in her eyes!

No.

No, that wasn't right.

Her fingers clawed at the stuff covering her sight.

It was dark red. Clotted.

An eye, pupil twitching back and forth.

Blood.

Duane with his head yawning open as if someone had tried to split it with an axe, chopped open.

Duane was in front of her. So was his brother, Cliff. They were lying on the floor, naked except for the blood.

There was something between their legs. Two different somethings. Duane had a round something, a circular thing of neon brightness, and Cliff had a cylinder something, which despite the blood and shit that streaked it, was still bright yellow. Both were coated in the punctuation of death, commas and exclamation points of bright red.

Nadia knew what the objects were, but at the same time, she could not have named them, because her brain refused to admit that they -or, rather "it"; they were the same something- should have been there. The context made it impossible to grasp.

Duane and Cliff looked like they were kissing, their faces mashed together, arms gripping each other by the biceps. They were lying on their bellies in a spreading stain that made Nadia think about her stomach full of wine-dyed vomit waiting to come up...

Duane's split skull was still yawning. Cliff didn't seem injured, at first, but then the there was so much blood that at first she hadn't seen that his throat had been hacked open.

It wasn't a spit-roast, in the end.

Close, but not quite.

If it was anything culinary, then surely it was a shish kebab.

Despite the context being insane, Nadia could finally name the thing that was thick as the fat end of a snooker cue that impaled both brothers on its six foot length, shunted up Duane's anus to bore straight through his body and emerge from his mouth, where the metal length of the thing then passed into Cliff's, stretching his jaw wide and smashing in his teeth as it was shoved down his throat and guts to emerge smeared with blood and shit and interstitial fluids from between his buttocks...

It was a lollipop pole, the kind wielded by friendly men and women across the country, who aided schoolchildren in crossing the road to their education.

The edges of the sign were sharp and caked in blood and hair. It had been used as an axe to split a skull, and a blade to slit a throat.

And as if uncorked, Nadia puked.

FOUR

THERE WAS another fatality. Another hedgehog had been stamped into a gooey paste on that anonymous kitchen floor.

And another one's gone, and another one's gone, another one bites the dust!

Oh frig, now she was going to have that Queen song stuck in her head all day.

The new message had been waiting for Krissi when she switched her phone on. Most mornings she woke up just before six, and would spend the first few minutes of the day snug under the covers scrolling through her feed to see what the night owls and people she knew in other countries had been up to whilst she slept. After catching up on the details of other people's lives she was ready to get up and live her own, which would first involve rousing Sam and getting him ready for school before then visiting the clients she had lined up for the day.

And yes, some mornings she got to play "Punch or Anteater?"

But not this morning.

She had opened the first message to find that THE SCRIVENER had sent her another picture, so whoever he was, her ignoring him (thanks to the message thread being deleted, though she had not planned on replying anyway) hadn't dissuaded him.

Krissi frowned at the picture. One, two, three cakes had been ruined out of six, but there was more change in the setting than just another waste of food. Something else was off, but she couldn't quite place her finger on it. As the minutes passed and she couldn't name whatever the changed element was, the more she wished -almost wished- that her son hadn't deleted the previous message thread.

The Scrivener... what's that supposed to mean? Is it supposed to be scary, or some kind of clue? What IS a scrivener anyway?

She tapped it in and did a search on the word.

The entry on Wikipedia told her almost nothing;

"A scrivener (or scribe) was a person who could read and write or who wrote letters to court and legal documents. Scriveners were people who made their living by writing or copying written material."

Blah blah blah...

Scrolling down the list of search results, it was also apparently the name for some text-editing software, as well as the name for a dam and a glacier in Australia and Antarctica respectively.

"Bartleby the Scrivener"

She stopped scrolling. Something about that entry caught her eye, but as she stared at it nothing came to her. She read more of the entry... it was about a short story written by Herman Melville, the bloke who wrote Moby Dick.

She frowned at her phone, her bottom lip sticking out as she thought.

The bloke who wrote Moby Dick wrote a story about a scrivener... and somebody calling himself the Scrivener was sending her photos that she thought were going to be dick pics... was there some kind of play on words going on? Maybe. Possibly. She didn't know, but if there was she didn't get it. Mind you, she often didn't get jokes or clever wordplay. Her mind didn't work that way, which meant that whoever had sent her the photographs obviously didn't know her very well.

Or at all.

Which means it's looking more and more likely this is just some random creep who's building his way up to something... probably sending me the world's smallest, ugliest anteater!

That made her smile, and so doing she got up, ready to start hers and her son's day without having opened the other message she had received overnight.

*****

Krissi walked Sam to school, kissing him goodbye at the gate even though he disliked being touched; she had let him know long ago that the school gate kiss was non-negotiable.

She stopped only just long enough to exchange meaningless pleasantries with the two-faced bitches who also walked their kids to school and then stood around "nattering" for twenty minutes after the bell had rung.

The mummies on the bus go natter natter natter...

She knew what they said about her, behind her back, after having said good morning and made some passive-aggressive remarks disguised as a compliment, normally based around her age.

Only twenty, already has a kiddy in school, obviously a scrounger on loads of benefits, a slag, probably lining up the next baby already, probably wants a brown one this time...

They hated her, and she hated them, in that particularly British way whereby everyone knows it and no-one ever says it. They hated her because she was young, slim, and attractive. It was pretty simple; hate from envy mixed with vague notions of moral superiority that didn't stand up in the light of day. She hated them for reasons that weren't so simple; she hated them because, in some part of her mind, she agreed with them. She had had a kid too young, she had relied on the state, she had...

Krissi banished these thoughts from her mind by walking home quicker. For frigs sake, maybe the tiny little maisonette they lived in was council owned, so what? All her money was her own, and that was without help from Sam's dad, who truly was a waste of space... and maybe, yes, she had been far too young to become a mum, but hadn't she worked hard enough to provide him with everything, love, clothes, a roof and food? There was no need to feel shame or to seek anyone else's approval, especially not the lumpy, sallow faced creatures at the school gates.

The truth was, Sam had been the making of her. Having him at the age of fourteen had forced her to grow up, to end the drink and the drugs and...

She stopped walking, breathing heavily. The air was thick with car fumes, a busy world of cars and lorries on the main road.

Every frigging morning I do this to myself. And every morning I promise myself this will be the last time for this little talk, so listen up, bitch, because I ain't going to say this again... until tomorrow, anyway. YOU got your hairdressing qualification. YOU built up a list of regular clients, and YOUR child never goes hungry or cold.

YOU are not YOUR MOTHER.

Ah, there it was, the all-important magic phrase.

And with it said loudly and clearly in her own mind, she started walking again, already mentally arranging her workday ahead.

FIVE

THE THING that squeezed its head through the letterbox was late, but it was huge, so she forgave it.

A stupid old joke popped into her head;

What do you do if an elephant comes through your cat flap? Swim for it!

It was a little unprofessional though, sticking your cock through the client's letterbox, even if it was their birthday...

Ever since the accident, Celina's world had shrunk and become more and more compartmentalised. People in particular were easy to fix with labels.

Men, for example. Before her accident at the age of eighteen, she knew exactly what they wanted and understood why they wanted it, and it was simple; she was gorgeous and they wanted to fuck her. From a tubby childhood, she had emerged from the chrysalis of adolescence as an absolute stunner pursued relentlessly by the opposite sex.

But then, after her accident, when she lost not only her ability to walk but also any chance of creating new life within herself, men still wanted one thing from her, but now the motivation was not so simple and her interactions with the opposite gender came down to assigning them one of three different character labels; chancers, martyrs, and bucketheads.

Chancers saw her as an easy lay; she's in a wheelchair, she'll be a pushover, she must be gagging for it because no-one else is willing to give her crippled up pussy a poke...

Martyrs were basically chancers who were so delusional they had actually talked themselves into believing they were doing her a favour; poor lass, bet nobody ever chats her up, bet most other blokes steer well clear of her, I'll show her she's still able to pull...

And *bucketheads* were those odd individuals who actually had "fuck a cripple" on their bucket list... or who quickly added it on seeing her.

Bastards.

Her friends had tried to convince her that they would still be able to go out and have fun like they had before, that nothing had really changed. But too many night outs for dinner, or to go to a pub or a club, which started with trying to negotiate her chair through a world made for people on two legs - restaurants with tables so close together that diners had to move to let her through; pubs where she couldn't see over the bar to order drinks- and ended with a chancer or a martyr or a buckethead making the same inane comments or asking the same asinine questions as they tried their pathetic best to talk her into... into what exactly? Catching a specially adapted taxi to a hotel with sufficient disabled access to get nasty... or a roll into the handicapped toilets for a blowjob she was now permanently at just the right height to administer?

Bastards.

Gradually the night outs became more infrequent, and Celina was not so mired in bitterness or cynicism that she didn't recognise that it was half her fault and half her friends'; it was precisely because she had become bitter and cynical that nobody wanted to hang around that. Increasingly, her friend's attitudes which had begun with the best intentions had turned into a sense of duty, then pity, and finally reached the point where they were so hacked off that they were able to jettison both their guilt and their friendship with her.

Celina discovered she was okay with this.

But still...

Bastards.

So now she stayed in, and when she got the itch that had to be scratched -incapable of having children though it was, her plumbing was otherwise in full working order- she simply did what she did when she got hungry.

She ordered in.

*****

Celina had been eighteen. She had been in college studying interior design, and living her best live, experimenting with drugs and her sexuality. The whole world was opening up in front of her and she loved it.

After a particularly intense few months of work, her tutor had proposed that the whole class ought to take a trip to Paulton's Park, an amusement park just outside Southampton. They could hire a mini-bus and get there early, on the Friday before half-term so that they would have the place mostly to themselves, because it was early in the season and they would have only just opened up after being in shut-down all winter; they only opened in the week before the half-term as a way of getting everything ready, making sure the rides were in tip-top condition for the start of the holiday season...

One of the rides, a mid-size roller-coaster called the Black Rainbow, was not in tip-top condition.

A stationary test car had failed at the base of the first rise, and it was into this that a group of half the interior design students had crashed at thirty-four miles per hour. In what one newspaper tactlessly reported as a "miracle", only one of the students received any major injuries, with the rest suffering only minor abrasions, contusions, and shock. The one student who had received a major injury was Celina.

A miracle.

She lived in a bungalow paid for by the massive pay-out she had received from the theme park. It was long and skinny, with her living room and kitchen at one end, the bedroom and bathroom at the other, connected by a long open space that was too wide to properly be called a hallway. Her home was sparsely furnished, because she spent most of her time in her motorised wheelchair, and furniture had become the bane of her existence. Her parents came around once a week, but that was only a bargain she had reached with them after a lot of arguing; she wanted to retain her independence, they were worried about her, and only a lengthy shouting match at one of the therapy sessions the theme park had paid for as part of her rehabilitation had been able to set what she came to think of as their "visitation rights."

Celina just wanted to be left alone whilst she figured out what the fuck she wanted to do with her fucked up life.

Well, not always alone...

She was able to see her front door from the living room, and thus the cock that was rammed through the letterbox.

Celina had been watching a wildlife documentary about life under the arctic ice sheet. She looked at the cock, then back at the starfish eking out a thin existence on the arctic seabed. She pressed a button, and the struggling starfish were replaced by the feed from the security camera outside her front door.

She almost laughed aloud. In shock, rather than amusement.

I asked for a man in uniform...

Actually, she wondered if she shouldn't be a bit hacked off.

A fireman, a copper, something like that for fucks sake...

She liked a little role play, but if this was the agency's idea of a joke they really didn't know their number one client very well.

Not that Celina knew she was their number one client, as she wouldn't admit to just how often she "ordered in" a little male company. Her general aura of anger and simmering bitterness made introspection something she little practised, but if she had been able to perform an examination of the full contents of her head, she might have realised that her desire for a man in uniform was because a fireman or a copper who came in and got naked for you on your 21st birthday were generally arranged by the good friends you had to celebrate the date with in fun, trashy style.

The doorbell rang again.

The image wasn't great, and it was taken from above head height and just to one side -the camera hidden so that any caller wouldn't know they were being observed- but it was quite clear that the figure on her doorstep was dressed like a lollipop man; hi-vis trench-coat to keep him warm and seen on a cold morning, the peaked cap, the bloody great big pole that said STOP CHILDREN on it...

Celina had a very brief moment of psychic sensitivity.

Something was wrong with this picture, and she should not answer the door. She should, in fact, call the police and pretend she wasn't in until they arrived.

Unfortunately, the anger which was a permanent part of her life since the day she had almost been killed blotted out the instinctive reaction. Instead, she tried to figure out what exactly was amiss.

She looked back up the hallway. The cock hung there like an elephant's trunk.

She looked at the screen.

Unless the caller was so well endowed he was literally bigger than a horse, the man outside was standing too far away from the letterbox for that to be his cock.

He was standing with the toes of his boots just on the mat. His trench-coat obscured her view of the door, but that meant his crotch was a foot away from the slot her post tumbled through.

She looked back at the cock.

It was at least eight inches. Flaccid.

Twelve inches, plus eight...

That's not even fucking human.

At that moment, the caller lost his grip, and the severed sexual organ slithered through the slot to fall with a wet plop on the floorboards.

Celina stared.

It had fallen in a curled up pile, like a cartoon dog turd. The end that should have been attached to a groin was ragged skin and glossy raw muscle bleeding out, a rill of blood running into the crack between the floorboards.

The letterbox flap opened, a brace of black gloved fingers pushing it up from the outside as the other hand squeezed two more objects through that fell to the boards on either side of the ripped off cock with soft little thuds. They were creamy and streaked with red, and about the size of eyes.

But they weren't eyes.

Testicles.

Movement from the corner of her eye was all that allowed Celina to look away from the disgusting sight of a man's destroyed sexual organs sat in smears and puddles of blood, a movement on the giant television screen that was still switched to the camera outside her front door. A camera that was supposed to be secret, but evidently was not, as the visitor in the lollipop man uniform had reached up and twisted it down and to the left to show what had been just out of view.

A man dressed as a copper lay in an untidy heap. His stab vest had been unable to prevent whatever had nearly cut his head off, neck open all the way to exposed vertebra, and his trousers pulled down to expose what was now a bloody crater where his sex had once been.

Celina screamed when the television and the lights both died at once, plunging the whole bungalow into darkness.

*****

Shock –caused by the carnage pushed through the letterbox, the turn her planned evening of joyless sex had taken, the sudden darkness-meant that some time passed before Celina realised she had to do something. Seconds, minutes… how long had she sat in her chair in the dark, her mind a blank?

I have to… I have to…

Run? Hide? Call for help? What did you do when there was a killer outside your house?

Her anger stepped up to take charge.

Call the fucking police you numpty, then get to the kitchen, get a knife!

Yes.

She kept her phone in a small holster attached to the right arm of her chair, just next to the motorised controls. She plucked it out and immediately dropped it as fear and adrenaline made her fingers twitch.

Fucking idiot!

It hit the floorboards with a double thump, bouncing in some direction, but with the lights off, who knew where exactly.

Shit shit shit!

Having spent the greater part of the last two years of her life in the bungalow, she knew from the loudness and the direction of the sound that the window which was suddenly broken was the one in her bedroom.

He's coming in!

She had a grabber, attached to the left arm of her chair. She used it for those occasions when she dropped stuff, like if she was cooking, and a split bag of salad potatoes sent a half dozen spuds tumbling to the ground. With trembling fingers she pulled it out, clamping it in one angry fist and then jabbing the clawed end down to the dark floor on her right.

The claw was made of semi-rigid plastic covered in rubber to make it easier to grip pretty much anything, but the first thing they touched was just bare board. She jabbed to the left, tapped more floorboards, then randomly darted back to the right and still found nothing.

Think this through, stop flapping about and be systematic!

Right, yes. She tapped the claw down once more and began to draw a circle on the ground. Encountering no resistance, she slowly began to expand the circle, spiralling around and around very carefully, hoping to make contact with her phone but not so violently she sent it skittering further away from where she was.

She heard the door of her bedroom. It made this tiny creak when it was about one third open. That tiny creak had always been one of those vague annoyances that everyone has in their life that wasn't big enough to ever get around to doing anything about, but now, in the dark, unable to move until she found her phone, that creak made all the skin on her arms and back prickle with goose bumps and her stomach gave a sour lurch of fear.

Her hand began to shake.

No! Find your fucking phone and this will all be over! Find it!

The thought was completely absurd of course, but it became her entire world, as if her twenty one years on this planet had all been preparation for the simple act of here and now picking up her phone with the stupid little grabber she needed for everyday tasks because she lived alone, having driven everyone else out of her life…

If the rat-panic of the moment hadn't completely consumed her, that thought would have made her weep.

She expanded the circle, even though she could no longer stop her hand shaking,

From the far end of the wide hallway, from where her bedroom was, came a sound both familiar and out of place.

The creak of her door was one thing, and this other sound was quite similar to it, but at the same time…

The squeak came again, and then a sound of something heavy slumping.

The squeak was the sound of a little used axle, a ball bearing that needed oil.

The slump was the sound of a body settling in.

She saw what happened in her mind's eye, saw the killer in the lollipop man outfit unfolding it and then sitting down in it…

…but what the fuck is he using my back-up chair for?

She had a standard push along wheelchair, just in case of emergencies, such as if her motorised chair developed a problem and she needed to call out an engineer to fix it. It was always folded up and leaning against the wall of her bedroom next to the door.

But the lunatic who had killed and castrated her evening's escort had just unfolded it, and was now sitting in it, at the far end of the pitch black hallway.

The claw nudged something, the little vibration running up the rod of its body and into her hand. Her phone!

Her attention flew from the mystery of the invader's strange activity back to concentrating wholly on using the grabber to secure purchase on the oblong object on the ground and bringing it up to her lap.

Miraculously, her hand stopped shaking, her concentration was so strong, so utterly focused, and in less than ten seconds she had her phone back.

Her fingers flew, lighting it up, tapping the app to access its dial screen, thumb stabbing the number nine three times…

Celina had it to her ear and was waiting for the second ring to end when the lights came back on.

Her eyes had been fixed on the point where he was, at the other end of the hall, as if she could see him in the dark, hold him there, hold him back with the strength of her unseeing gaze.

The light caused her to blink, momentarily stunning her.

He had started wheeling down the hall as the call was answered.

"Hello, emergency services, do you require police, fire, or ambulance?" asked the almost monotone female operator.

"I…" Celina squinted.

His face was unclear, her vision too blurred, but she could make out what he was doing. Sat in her back up chair, his hi-vis trench coat a blur of glaring colour. He had his lollipop stick held clamped under his armpit, the sign bit behind him, the pointed end towards her. He had to clamp it under his armpit to hold it in place as he rapidly spun the chair's wheels, gaining speed as he came towards her. Getting faster…

"Hello, emergency services, do you require police, fire, or ambulance?" asked the almost monotone female operator again.

Celina had been talking since she was 18 months old, but all of a sudden those words meant nothing to her. The absurdity of everything that had happened in the past fifteen or twenty minutes – really, has it only been that long since this fucking nightmare began- had seemingly destroyed her ability to comprehend her own language.

He was pumping the wheels hard, getting faster.

A wheel rolled right over one of the escort's testicles, which burst like a zit, sending a comet tail of semen across the floorboards.

The end of the lollipop pole, pointing at her, as thick as a snooker cue.

Nothing made sense.

Jousting. That's what it's called. Like knight's did back in olden times.

Her own voice in her head sounded mildly interested.

Blinking, she saw the lollipop man's face at last. It came into focus just long enough for her to recognise it, but between that recognition and the moment she died, she wouldn't be able to place where she knew it from.

"Hello, this is emergency services, are you…"

"It's my birthday," Celina told the voice, and then lollipop man let go of the wheels to grab the pole and brace it as the sharp end punched through Celina's dressing gown, straight through her left breast, her ribs, and popped her lung.

What followed was a series of isolated moments. Not pictures, but small clips like animated gifs as Celina's shocked brain began the process of shutting down.

Blackness.

Here was the man pushing back, feet shoving against the floor, tugging the sharp end of the pole out of her chest in a welter of hot, thick blood.

Blackness.

Here was a brief flashback to the accident, that other great defining moment of her life filled with fear and shattering pain.

Blackness.

Here was the man discarding the pole, reaching with black gloved fingers to touch the hole in her chest.

Blackness.

Here was some time in hospital. She couldn't place exactly when it was, not even from what she heard herself telling the nurse attending her, as during her recovery, knowing what her life was now reduced to, she had often expressed a wish to simply fucking die.

Blackness

Here was the lollipop man pulling out his erection *–Jesus Christ what's wrong with his cock?-* and teasing the end of it into her chest. The tip found the rip in her lung, and then the cock was sliding into the mucous slick bag that had provided her with oxygen her whole life.

He fucked the wound until he came in her lung.

She coughed, and coughed, and coughed.
Until she could taste spunk.
And here she actually did die.
Blackness forever.

SIX

MOST OF her clients were in the late fifties or quite a bit older, many of them unable to get out to a hairdresser on their own. With the older ones especially, Krissi might be one of the few people they saw from week to week, so she often got them in any shopping they might need, and spent longer on fixing up their hair then was strictly necessary because they had as much a need for conversation as a trim.

And, she had even admitted to herself, one evening alone at home thinking about the past whilst drinking rum, it was good for her as well; her ladies had lifetimes of experience and stories to pass along, and had become for Krissi a sort of committee of mother figures.

She did not have a car. There wasn't really a space to park one in her road, or any of the adjoining ones, but she couldn't afford to run one anyway. She had a sturdy rucksack that she carried her supplies in, and walked to each of her ladies that she could, catching the bus to any who were further out than a half hour from home. Apart from when it was absolutely hammering down, or in the worse extremes of temperature, she enjoyed marching all over the place. It kind of made her feel a bit like she was in medieval times, a wanderer plying her trade where she could. That, and it also kept her in great shape; there were times at the school gate she would have been delighted to explain that it wasn't just youth on her side, but the fact that she didn't drive her boy to school in a frigging Land Rover which was responsible for why she did not have bingo wings as every other mum seemed to.

Her last client for the day was Mrs Knight.

Mrs Knight was even more agitated today than she usually was.

"Isn't it a wicked world, Christine? Makes you afraid to go to sleep at night, for fear of waking up and finding it even worse the next morning!"

Krissi was lathering her hair, hoping that a gentle scalp massage would calm her down.

"Now why do you say that Mrs Knight? It was beautiful first thing today."

The older woman shook her head. Krissi gently restrained her.

"I don't mean the weather, I mean the world! Don't tell me you didn't hear about that horrible murder?"

"I can't say as I did, I don't really follow the news. My boy loves it though, for some reason."

Mrs Knight took no time in telling Krissi all about it, though the truth was, having only been discovered the day before, and with the police being cagey as they were with all such investigations, there wasn't much to tell, just that some poor disabled girl had been attacked and killed in her own home on the other side of town.

"...so that's three now! Three murders in as many months! First that rugby fellow and his brother, and now this lass, attacked in her own home! And come to think of it, that was the same with those brothers, wasn't it, they lived in a flat together... Your own home, you aren't even safe in the one place you should feel safe!"

Krissi's fingers had stopped massaging shampoo into the woman's hair momentarily when she'd mentioned the brothers. God, that was right, she'd forgotten, the twins, she'd gone to primary school with them. When she'd first heard about it two months ago -from Mrs Knight, in fact- she'd felt a sort of numb shock, something like pins and needles, only through her entire body. She hadn't see Duane or his brother in years, but they'd been a part of her gang when they were all kids in St. Edward the Confessor's. Hearing that somebody from your childhood had been murdered was surreal, like hearing somebody from a nursery rhyme had been killed.

No, that wasn't right. But at the same time, it was; so strange, and so awful.

Being reminded about the twins put a dampener on the rest of her day. Even Sam noticed that she wasn't chatty on the way home. He actually asked her what was wrong. When he did so, Krissi almost burst into tears, and was astonished to find she felt that way. It was all such a big mix-up of different things; pictures in her head of the twins when they were all kids together and now her own son, almost the age of those boys in her mind's eye, worried about her even though he found talking hard. He was such a sweet boy, and Mrs Knight was correct, it was such a wicked world.

But it wasn't until later that evening, Sam tucked up and sleeping, Krissi in her own bed, on her phone, anxiously scanning through the news that she recalled what else Mrs Knight had said;

Your own home, you aren't even safe in the one place you should feel safe!

She tried to stop herself, but in the end she couldn't. Krissi got up out of the warmth of her bed and went and checked that the front door was locked, and that all the windows were secure.

When she got back to bed, she noticed she had a new notification in her message box.

Her stomach rolled over, slow and greasy.

It'll just be a frigging dick pic. Come on, you average eight a week, and so far you've only had four, five? You're due a couple of Punch's...

But it was not a dick pic, or even what she had not admitted to herself she feared it would be.

Not a dick pic, and not another message from the Scrivener.

The message she hadn't opened that morning had tripled itself. Three messages, all from the same unrecognised number, and now file attachments, so now anteaters or Punches or smashed cakes.

CHRISTINE SKELTON??? WENT TO SAINT ED CONFESSER???

ITS ADELE PHIPPS WE HAV TO TALK

THERE DEAD IT WAS THE LOLLIPOP MAN

*****

She looked like shit.

Drugs. It's got to be drugs.

Krissi felt a brief surge of emotions upon seeing her old friend. There was shock of course, and empathy, and disgust.

And fear.

The fear was complicated and nebulous. It was not only composed of the dread she'd had waiting for this meeting, but also now mixed with the disgust and empathy at seeing Adele a wreck; Krissi knew she was looking at a life that might have been hers, if it hadn't been for Sam.

Adele had been staring down at her cup when she'd opened the door of the Art Deco café, her feet drumming under the table with the nervous energy of someone strung out. Krissi had a chance to observe her old friend for maybe three seconds, before Adele looked up and clocked her, the scarecrow face suddenly grinning a grin that had holes in it.

Krissi walked over.

"Adele?"

"Hi," the scarecrow was half standing, reaching for her old friend's hand and grabbing it in both of hers. Her hands were too cold, too thin, her grasp desperate rather than welcoming. "Christine, wow, hi, thank you, thank you for coming."

Krissi sat. Adele leaned forward, getting too close. Her breath was bad, like sweet burning plastic.

"Thank you so much, you're looking so good, I've been so scared, first it was the twins and then..."

A waitress appeared, and Adele suddenly shut up her twitchy rambling, an automatic reaction to keep silent when any sort of authority was near. Krissi ordered something, she didn't exactly know what, so shocked was she at the messed up creature her childhood friend had become.

When the waitress was gone, Adele closed her eyes and rubbed her temples with the fingers of each hand.

"Right, right, I know what I must sound like, I know what I look... OK. Be normal. Conversation." Her eyes opened again, laced with broken blood vessels but firmly focused on Krissi. "Hello Christine. Long time, yeah?"

"Yes, it has been a long time," said Krissi. After primary school, most of the Skeleton Gang had gone on to the single sex Catholic secondary schools that St Edward's was a feeder for, but Krissi's mum had realised she'd have to spend money on bus fare for that to happen, money that could have gone on booze, so Krissi had gone to Thornbee High School, much closer to home. And there she had gone completely off the rails, starting down a path of truancy, delinquency, and substance abuse which had only been arrested by falling pregnant to a twenty-two year old who bought her and her friends vodka

The silence stretched.

Frig this...

“Adele, I came because... I don’t know really. I should have just deleted all your messages. Most of them made no sense.”

But then you claimed you knew who killed the twins... and Celina.

The waitress returned, bringing a cup of mint tea. Krissi wondered why the frig she’d ordered mint tea. She paid, and the waitress made a point of asking if they needed anything else. The look on her face when she glanced at Adele suggested she wondered if someone had trod in dog shit and brought the smell in.

When the woman was gone Adele sipped her coffee. When she spoke, she spoke to the drink.

“Christine, I am what I look like. I’m all fucked up. And I know I’m kind of in and out at times, sketchy as fuck. I know. But I meant what I told you. The Lollipop Man killed them all,” and then she looked up and her eyes were very clear. “And he’s going to kill us.”

Krissi didn’t know what to do with her hands.

“You mean the man who used to see us across the road, at school?”

“Yes.”

“But he died, didn’t he? I remember hearing that...”

Adele said nothing.

“The rumour was that he killed himself.”

“He did.”

There was an empty moment.

"If he killed himself," said Krissi, "then how can he possibly be murdering our old friends? Adele... look, I'm going to go now. It was nice... no, I won't lie, it wasn't nice seeing you. You look like your dying. I don't know why I came."

Adele's thin, cold hands leapt across the table and grabbed Krissi's. The sudden movement and the intense look on the woman's haggard, gaunt face stopped Krissi in the act of getting up.

"It's the lollipop man, Christine," she whispered. "It is him. He killed Duane and Cliff and Celina on their 21st birthdays. You know what twenty one used to be? It used to be the age when you officially became an adult. But he's not going to let us become adults. On my birthday he will kill me, and on your birthday he will kill you."

Krissi saw the waitress at a table on the other side of the room watching them both. They locked eyes. The waitress cocked her head slightly... but Krissi shook hers.

For frigs sake, just... frig, humour her.

"OK Adele," she said, pushing the other woman's hands back slowly. "OK. For the moment, let's just go over what you've said. You believe..."

"I know!"

"...that the man who used to help us cross the road when we were children, a man who is dead, has killed our old friends and is going to kill us.Fine. Before I go on, can you at least understand that what you said sounds frigging potty?"

Adele nodded.

"Yes, it sounds like the crazy shit you'd expect a homeless junkie to say," she said reasonably.

"Right. Cool. But that leaves a load of questions. Like first, why would a lollipop man who I barely remember want to hurt me, or you, or the twins? Why?"

Adele was frowning. The extra lines it added to her face made her look closer to forty than twenty. God, what was she on that had ravaged her?

"You don't remember what we did to him?"

"I don't think about my childhood. It wasn't a happy time..."

...oh my god I've just realised Adele you've got the same look the look my mum had only with her it was vodka...

"...and I don't think of it as part of my own life anymore."

Adele blinked stupidly.

"So you don't remember the stuff we used to say to him? You don't remember that you used to call him a paedophile? To his face?To the teachers, and parents? Nice Mr Bartleby, who used to call all the kids his hedgehogs, because it was his job to stop us getting squashed on the road?"

Krissi heard the name and her heart was caught between two beats.

Adele blinked.

"We drove him to it. He killed himself because of us. Because of you."

Krissi couldn't move.

Bartleby... The Scrivener... like that story by that bloke who wrote *Moby Dick*.

"When's your birthday?" Adele asked, a sick grin on her face, exposing how many teeth she was missing. Jesus, she was the same age as Krissi, but she looked like a corpse! "I seem to remember you and me and Tony had them all close together. We were the smallest in our year, remember? That's why we started hanging around together. When's your birthday Christine?"

She began to croon;

"Happy birthday to you!
Squashed tomatoes and stew!
Blood and butter in the gutter,
Happy birthday to you!"

The waitress was coming over, looking ready to bash heads together. Krissi was retreating, throwing money on the table.

Adele started to laugh, a cracked junkie cackle.

"Don't you remember?" she asked, laughing and laughing. "Don't you remember... I was the youngest!"

*****

Two weeks later, when Krissi had finally convinced herself that the junkie was full of shit, she got another pic from the Scrivener.

Another smashed hedgehog cake.

SEVEN

IN A crowd who wore leather and latex, spiked collars and choke chains, gimp masks, pony harnesses, and every other imaginable kind of fetish gear, the figure of the lollipop man stood out. But everybody had their own kink, and whilst his was rare, the lollipop man would be tolerated. All were tolerated.

The music was loud and the lights were dim. He descended into the club with the brim of his cap pulled low, his lollipop carried at his side as if he were striding out into traffic to make the road safe for schoolchildren. He attracted a certain amount of attention, but not as much as he would have if the crowd in *Hush Hush* hadn't liked to consider themselves jaded, and so deliberately affected that they were not jarred at the sight of such an unknown kink.

There were exceptions, though.

One young man who was high on the latest chemical of the streets saw the Lollipop Man pass by the booth he was slumped in, the drug's effects warping the lollipop man's hi-vis trench-coat and traffic stopping sign into a hyper-kinetic, twenty first century nightmare version of the grim reaper.

The young man burst into tears. Even when one of his friends asked him what was wrong, he couldn't articulate what he had seen.

Tony Peacock didn't see him enter, and wouldn't have been alarmed if he had. Tony wasn't on any of the mainstream social media networks, and so the attempts an old school friend had made to contact him had failed; none of the Tony Peacock's who had received messages about Mr Bartleby or the Scrivener had a clue about them, or anything to do with the Skeleton Gang who had once attended St Edward the Confessor Primary School.

It was the evening of his twenty-first birthday, and as he had passed the old threshold into adult hood, all his friends at the Hush Hush club were going to give him a twenty one gun salute.

After pass the parcel, of course.

Everyone was naked save for their party hats, cardboard cones decorated with pictures of clowns, with thin elastic straps that hooked under the chin.

The bar on the far side of the room held the remains of the party feast they'd all put away before the games had begun. Paper platters of sausage rolls and pizza slices, bowls of crisps and peanuts, chocolate mini rolls, and biscuits had been decimated by the fully grown adult men indulging in the kind of fare normally enjoyed by five-year-olds... but it was what Tony had wanted, according to Clem, the sort of party his strict parents had never let him have as a kid.

Old Clem, who was in his late forties and therefore a queen of some years standing, had explained everything to Tony. Young master Peacock, as old Clem called him, was still wet behind the ears, and needed taking under his wing.

Tony wasn't naive, far from it. He recognised the situation for what it was, but it was okay by him. Old Clem had become a father figure to replace his own biological father, who had disowned him along with the rest of his hard-line Catholic family at the age of seventeen when Tony had come out... a father figure who just happened to fuck him, whenever he choked down enough Viagra to get a stiffy. A father figure who owned his own fetish club, and loved to flaunt his trophy boy-toy. He dress Tony in a silk posing pouch, keeping things minimalist, and in doing so, drew all attention to the one thing that really made him stand out. The pouch was skin tight, not just because it was cut that way, but because of what it was barely able to restrain.

But what made Tony such a big deal was also his biggest secret.

All the regular's at *Hush Hush* knew that the young man on the arm of the club's owner had a bulge so big that it practically had gravity; you met Tony, your eyes were drawn downwards, dragged by the sheer bulk of that posing pouch that seemed stuffed close to bursting point with baking potatoes.

Young man Peacock was know to have an impressive dick, but it was the sheer size of his ball sack that made him a legend.

It was on this that most of his friends, ex-lovers, and "fans" were focusing as they masturbated.

They'd already been in a circle after playing pass-the-parcel. All that was needed was for the birthday boy to scoot into the centre.

He was sat cross legged on the floor of one of the champagne room, one of the private chambers. His cock and balls were cradled in his lap, completely shaved, the whole effect something like huge eggs in a nest with a bald bird squatting on them, all made of flesh. He had discarded his pouch and was massaging his enormous genitals with baby oil as twenty-one men in various stages of undress masturbated in a circle around him, their cocks the meat spokes on a wheel with him at the hub.

"Think of it as an official initiation into the club's inner circle," was how Clem put it.

He was one of the spokes. He'd gotten some kind of semi-legal, ultra cock stiffening drug smuggled over from Thailand for the occasion.

At first, Tony hadn't been too keen on the idea and was only going along with it because of peer-pressure. And besides, he wanted to stay on Clem's good side; he had a cushy life, as the older man kept him in pocket money and out of regular employment. But now he found himself thoroughly enjoying the sight of so much engorged meat surrounding him, being worked by eager fists, fuelled by a lust for him. They were all getting off because of him, because of how sexy he was, how much they wanted him. It was like the high he got off of parading around the club in his pouch, but far stronger. He'd always known he had a love for exhibitionism, but had not known this would extend this far.

Clem had been trying to persuade him to do some online cam-boy stuff, and now, with the sense of power he felt... maybe he'd do it.

"Oh boys, just look at you all," he moaned in an affected voice, breathy and wide eyed. "To think, all that hard meat is just for little old me!"

"Fuck off with the Marylin Monroe act Tony," grunted Reuben, to Tony's left. "I'm a gnat's chuff away from the vinegar strokes."

Several of the other men laughed.

Tony shuffled around on his bum until he was facing Reuben.

Reuben didn't have much in his hand, but he over-compensated for that with the kind of body that looked like an anatomy lesson. Every lean muscle was perfectly defined, including a six pack which was so perfect it could have been cast out of plastic. The two facts of his small cock and perfect torso had earned him a nickname.

Tony hefted his ball sack and smiled coyly.

"Oh, sorry Action Man, didn't mean to put you off your stroke!"

Reuben swore at him again, and began to frantically stroke himself.

More laughter.

"Right, that's it, I'm getting the first shot! Get your mouth open Peacock!"

"Look who you're calling pea-cock Action Man..."

Tony drew out the last syllable as a kind of groan from the back of his throat as he opened his mouth, stuck out his tongue, and tilted his head back.

The red faced Reuben stumble-shuffled forward out of the ring of masturbating men, his hand whipping back and forth as fast as his wrist allowed, the end of his stunted cock popping in and out of his fist.

Then Clem came forward as well

"Fuck off Action Man, if anyone's drawing first blood, it's me!" he declared, jacking his long, skinny penis.

"Sword fight!" said someone, which got another laugh.

Tony raised his eyebrows twice, looking at his sugar daddy with his mouth open like he was about to take communion. The double-lift was an acknowledgement, and an encouragement.

Both men were now stood in front of him, their cocks at right angles as they frantically worked their inches. The other men stood around started calling out banter, declaring who they were betting on, encouraging their favourites who they picked because of long standing feuds or friendships, all whilst each still beating their meat.

"Go to it, Clem, show 'em experience is the name of the game!"

"Blow your load Reuben, blow your load!"

Tony hefted his own erection, slowly easing his fingers up and down the shaft as his other hand massaged the enormous swelling of his ball sack, the skin distended over what could have been a filling of two grapefruits.

Clem wasn't a spring chicken, but he was not the kind of bloke who would ever consider just letting it all go; he still worked out hard and kept his tan tastefully topped up, and only laughter lines and a touch of distinguishing silver in his hair revealed that he was twice his boy-toy's age.

Looking up at him like this, Tony realised that he truly did love the old fuck.

Maybe... maybe he should propose soon... before the secret got out...

Things couldn't go on like they were forever. His doctor had warned him.

Clem's eyes were fixed on his. Reuben was looking at the eggs in their nest as Tony throttled the mama bird.

The air was heady with testosterone and aftershave and sweat and alcohol fumes.

And every cock in the room was hard for *him*, the spunk in all their balls was bubbling and getting ready to spew forth because they were crazy in lust for *him*.

That thought, a clearly spoken truth, was enough to trigger Tony first, a surprise and sudden ejaculation before any of his birthday admirers. His cock was suddenly spurting in his fist, sending up ivory pearls of semen that fell splattering back onto his own grossly swollen scrotum.

He held onto himself, gasping and unable to articulate the sensation of the most powerful orgasm he had ever had.

He threw back his head and managed one word;

"Fuck!"

"Oh shit, Tony, oh shit that's..." said Clem, before he lost it, shooting slim ropes of spunk towards his boy-toy's mouth.

Tony felt it hit his face, and jerked as another wave of ecstasy pulsed through him. He lapped at the semen that slathered his chin, groaning.

Reuben lost it.

"Fuck fuckfuck!" he snarled, shaking a thick stream of cum out of his cock, firing gobs of the stuff over Tony's cheeks.

It was like a chain reaction.

As the three at the centre each orgasmed, so the other men waiting around in a wide circle felt themselves suddenly right on the edge, eagerly stumbling forward, sometimes bumping shoulders, almost a stampede to get forward and ready to unload on the birthday boy before they ended up shooting all over the floor instead.

Tony accepted every load like they were tributes, their quantity and consistency ranging from the likes of a sinus full of snot during a heavy cold, to discharges like water guns filled with egg white. Most of them landed on his face, splattering across his forehead and cheeks, lucky shots landing in his mouth or across his lips as he licked away the excess. Semen dripped from his ears onto his shoulders; mistimed ejaculations speckled his chest and belly and balls.

There was a cacophony of moans, groans, shouts of ecstatic release, yes, no, oh Christ, oh shit, so good, fuck me, and wordless exclamations that spoke volumes in the language of beasts.

All for Tony, a twenty-one gun salute.

*****

He'd gotten most of the cold cum off his face when somebody cleared their throat in the kissing booth.

Tony frowned. His reflection had silver pearls in its eyelashes, something Clem called "Valentine's Day Mascara." But he'd had to explain the joke to Tony, who knew nothing about American gangsters from decades ago.

Tony frowned because he'd thought he was alone in the champagne room's private toilets.

He'd retreated to clean himself up whilst the rest of the boys ordered in drinks and puffed away on post-orgy vape machines, cutting lines of coke and breaking open new vials of poppers so that the party could continue long into the night.

The bathroom had toilet facilities of course, including the sink which he was cleaning himself at, but it also had the kissing booth.

Clem had decided that the age old practice of "the glory hole" was a tradition that was dying out, and had intended to bring it up to date and also, in his words, "give it a lick of class." This was why the champagne room's private toilet had a pair of cubicles in it, though they weren't the kind constructed of cheap Formica, but rather were ornate cocobolo with tulipwood inserts. And rather than a hole crudely chipped through from one to the other beside the toilet roll holder, roughly at groin height, there was a specially designed gap about the size of a cat flap, lined with silk drapes, through which one willing participant could push his genitals to be manipulated by another, anonymously, in the next stall.

"Hello?" asked Tony. "Is there someone in there?"

Maybe he'd mistaken the sound of a cleared throat, which was why he asked, but there was no mistaking when a voice started to sing;

"*Happy birthday to yooouuuuu...*"

It was a thin, whispery sort of voice, a voice that was obviously being put on.

"*Squashed tomatoes and steeeewwww...*"

Tony grinned. Somebody was fucking around. Okay, he'd play along. Spunk still in his lashes and his cock still tingling from the mass circle jerk, he let himself into the left hand stall whose door was ajar.

"Jules?" Tony guessed as he entered the toilet stall, looking at the curtained glory hole, wondering what mouth might await on the other side. "Francis, is that you? Silky?" The voice kept speaking as he guessed. "Seamus, I bet that's you, you promised me a birthday present after the salute, I thought you just meant some edibles!"

"*...in the gutter... happy birthday to yooouuu!*"

Was this the offer of a birthday present?

The silk drapes of the hole fluttered, as if someone had blown on them from behind, blown like they were putting out the candles on a cake.

Even after the epic orgasm he'd had, Tony found himself getting hard again, rising to the occasion. Anonymous sex, even if it was only oral, was right up his street, but not something he'd been able to indulge in since becoming Clem's bit of stuff.

Clem.

He couldn't. He'd never cheat on the older man. He wasn't that kind of guy.

And yet... he didn't make his apologies and leave. He didn't point out to the faceless mouth on the other side of the hole that he was spoken for, so thanks but no thanks.

The blood that had rushed from his brain to his cock was making it hard to form those words. The speech centre of his brain was starved of oxygen.

He wondered again who it was, on the other side. The little drapes ruffled again on anonymous breath.

Who could have snuck in without anyone else noticing? The doors to the champagne room had been locked for the exclusive birthday bash, so it could only have been one of the twenty-one guests who had just spent their fuck on his face.

And even if Tony hadn't noticed, he knew that Clem would have noticed. Clem liked to play the generous and care-free host, but you didn't end up the owner of a fetish club unless you were sharper than razors. That, and he was a jealous bastard; his policy on Tony, even as he flaunted the younger man off, was that all patrons were free to look, but none could touch... unless on his strict say-so.

The twenty-one gun salute had been a rare privilege for only his closest friends and most important enemies.

The politics amongst the queens of the fetish scene were complex, and the social etiquette even more so

But what this meant was, if someone was in here, they were so with Clem's knowledge... was it a birthday present then, from the older man? To let in an admirer in to give his boy a good time on the sly, so that no-one would lose face for the infidelity?

It had to be.

This flimsy justification was all Tony needed.

He grinned widely as he eased his erection and then his enormous scrotum through the silk drapes of the glory hole, a thrill racing up his spine as he pushed his genitals into the presence of the unknown on the other side of the partition.

Seconds passed.

Then, fingers tickled him, lightly, a dancing touch along the top of his shaft.

A hand wrapped around him.

He sighed.

The hand squeezed.

He groaned.

The other hand gently cupped his balls, hefted the weight of him, let them drop again as if astonished by their weight.

"Yeeaahhh," he breathed. "I know, I know, you can't believe 'em can you?"

The thought that there was actually nothing to be believed drifted lazily across his blood starved brain.

He waited for the mouth which would surely come next. Would lips engulf the fat plum of his glans, or would a tongue trace the awesome curve of his hanging grapefruits?

It was neither.

Something cut him.

"Shit!"

Instinctively, Tony tried to pull back, but the hand wrapped around his shaft suddenly turned into a flesh and bone vice, crushing him and making retreat impossible.

The cut was fast and quick, across his scrotum, left to right.

But as unexpected as the attack was, what came next was something he would never have conceived in a thousand years of nightmares.

Whatever had cut him had left a gash big enough for fingers to wiggle their way in, two fingers that plunged into his ball sack up to the knuckles.

They weren't surprised, those fingers.

They knew what they would find.

They hooked around the length of gut and in the next moment pulled backwards hard and fast, as if pulling the starter cord on an old petrol chainsaw.

dragging his intestines out of the ragged slit in his scrotum.

Tony's big secret was, quite literally, out.

At the age of seventeen, a full year kicked out of home and surviving by whoring himself, Tony found his jeans becoming tight. Clothes were a luxury when you lived on sofas and other people's exploitation, and at first he had taken the increasing size of his ball sack to be some kind of symptom of an STI. But when he eventually got the courage to head to the clinic, he discovered that in fact, he had a truly monstrous hernia, a hole in the membrane that cradled his intestines that had allowed an increasingly large loop of his guts to squeeze out of his abdomen and into the relatively empty space of his scrotum.

Incredibly, it wasn't painful, and hadn't interfered with any of the normal operations of a set of male genitals. He could fuck and he could piss just fine.

But it looked like he had balls the size of a horse.

The doctor at the clinic had told Tony that it would be a good idea to get the issue seen to sooner rather than later, and that if untreated complications were sure to occur... but Tony was young, dumb, and suddenly in possession of something which he could market.

Eventually his sack reached the natural limits of expansion, and Tony began to make himself a name as the young whore with the biggest balls of any man's most warped fantasies. It wasn't long before he became a part of the scene that had its spiritual home at Hush Hush... and then, by natural progression, he became the exclusive property of old Clemency.

And now, someone had cut open his nut-sack and was pulling out his guts like they were winning in a tug-of-war.

Tony would have screamed, except the sensation of feeling his intestines slithering out of him, rubbing against the sides of his testicles like a length of greasy rope, made his gorge rise. The pain was one thing, like the flame of a blow torch was playing back and forth across his genitals, but the sensation... it was horrifying on an almost spiritual level.

Tony braced his hands against the wall and vomited down himself, a churned up bellyful of sausage rolls, jammy dodgers, and smoky bacon crisps mixed together with bubble-gum flavour Panda Pop.

The splattering sound the flood made cascading onto the floor made the tugging stop for a moment... then it resumed, with gusto.

Tony slumped against the wall, spitting gobbets of mushed up crumbs, bracing himself on one forearm, gazing down at the purple ropes streaked with blood that were sliding out of his rapidly deflating scrotum. Of course, it was a loop, so it was two lengths, side by side, that were coming out. His cock dangled over the right hand side. With his free hand he grabbed at them, and felt them slither through his palm, greasy with bloody mucous. It was like trying to hold onto a bicycle's inner tube that was soaked in KY jelly.

He gripped tighter.

The tugging was halted.

With a numb detachment, as if he were watching someone else, Tony kept his tight grip on his guts and pushed himself back from the wall, pulling, the shuddering tension of the intestine-rope hard won, inch by inch, from his assailant.

He stepped backward, pulled harder.

The twin lengths of purple tubing were suddenly cut. Something hacked through them on the other side of the wall, the sudden release sending Tony staggering backwards. His heels slipped on his omit and he careened backwards, smashing against the opposite wall and sprawling out awkwardly in the confined space.

With his head crooked against the wall, he could see the mess between his legs.

It looked like he had three dicks, though two of them were the wrong colour and had ragged ends that were ejaculating shit.

Shock settled on him like someone had thrown a blanket rimed with frost over his vulnerable body.

He began to shiver.

He heard the toilet stall door next to his open.

Footsteps.

The door to his left eased open, just enough to admit a lollipop. A gloved hand gripped it.

A lollipop man's lollipop.

And wrapped around its length, wound onto it, was a large amount of Tony's intestines.

Then the lollipop man forced his whole body through the gap.

Tony had a great memory for faces.

He recognised the man.

He opened his mouth to say something.

The lollipop spun around in the man's hands and he pressed the circular head into Tony's open mouth. He was not gentle, and the edges had been sharpened. It chipped Tony's incisors and cut into the corners of his mouth.

Then, as if it were a spade and Tony's face was a patch of ground that was to be dug up, the lollipop man stomped on the back edge of his sign and chopped Tony's head in half, leaving only his lower jaw attached to his neck.

The lollipop man lifted up the upper half of the birthday boy's head on the lollipop's sign like it was a big chunk of turf he had dug up, and tipped it into the toilet.

Owing to the nature of a brain staying alive for nearly two minutes after the blood supply is cut off, Tony not only saw, but smelled exactly where he ended up, as the previous occupant had not flushed away a large sweet-corn studded shit.

EIGHT

AFTER THE murder of Tony Peacock, Krissi did something she never thought she would do.

But she had no choice. She could see absolutely no alternative.

After her encounter in the coffee shop with Adele she had tried to dismiss the insane nonsense from her mind; the idea that the lollipop man from their childhood, a man they had tormented, perhaps hounded to suicide, had come back from the dead to murder them on their twenty-first birthdays... that was the stuff of the worst frigging horror rubbish.

But then, she couldn't just dismiss the Scrivener, could she?

Bartleby the Scrivener.

Mr Bartleby, the lollipop man.

The hedgehog birthday cakes stamped into ruin.

He called the kids his hedgehogs...

Krissi knew what a shitty kid she had been. There wasn't a shop within three miles of her house she was allowed into because of nicking; she was taking drugs and drinking and giving blowjobs before she had even hit her teens. But she also knew it wasn't exactly her fault. After her dad had walked out when Krissi was barely a week old, her mum had taken little interest in anything outside of a bottle of vodka, to the point that Krissi actual found herself salivating when she smelled the stuff; her mum had been drinking hard even when she was breast feeding Krissi, which had hard-wired a Pavlovian response into her brain.

Her childhood belonged to someone else. Christine, not Krissi.

But she did remember the early days, with her gang, directing them in shoplifting, and the delicious sense of power that she got from saying the most awful things to the kindly lollipop man. She also vaguely remembered hearing that he had died, but not that he had killed himself.

The very idea made her sick. She wasn't that kid anymore. Having her own child had switched something in her mind, for the better.

Simply put, not long after the birth of Sam she had had a revelation. She was still drinking, still smoking shit and taking pills with her "friends" who gave her these things in exchange for sucking them off, and she resented the eerily quiet baby that had invaded her life. The revelation had come out of nowhere, a fully formed adult thought, a thought that was mature way beyond her years, born of a paradox.

The only reason she hadn't given up Sam to child services was because her mum had convinced them she would help raise him.

Her alcoholic mum.

The person, she realised in that incredibly bright moment of realisation, she hated most in the world.

The person she was turning into.

Overnight, she had nothing to do with her friends, who weren't friends, something she'd always known. She turned the focus of her life from herself to Sam, and as soon as she was able to, she left home.

It had taken a few years of living on her own, struggling to make something of herself, before she realised why she had reacted so violently; it was because her mum, with Sam around, had started to become the kind of mum she had always wanted as a kid... towards her grandson. When Krissi had kept going out to get fucked up, her mum had never been drunk when she came back, had stayed off the bottle so that she could properly care for Sam.

In a bizarre way, her revelation was partly based on the paradox that her own mum had found her maternal instinct -an instinct that had stretched little beyond buying Krissi new clothes every other year, and serving up the same burnt meal of fish fingers and oven chips every single night- because Krissi had begun the cycle of neglect with her own baby.

And at the very bottom, her reaction was really a simple one; jealousy.

Birthdays and Christmas were days when her mum was invited around to her home, and a few other times throughout the year, if Krissi was desperate, she'd leave Sam at her mum's for tea...

but never more than a couple of hours, and never overnight.

But now...

Yes, before Tony's death she had tried to dismiss what Adele had said as nonsense. Tried and failed, as there was the communications from the Scrivener, and her old friends were definitely dead. It would have been foolish to just dismiss it all out of hand, so she turned amateur Web detective.

She had located the stories of the deaths of the twins and Celina in various local and national press reports. The details were scant, as they always were, but the few facts stood out starkly enough. The twins and Celina had been murdered on their twenty-first birthdays. The nature of the killings, of course, were not explicitly given, and to date the police had no suspects, and no witnesses... though they were eager to trace the whereabouts of Nadia, the girlfriend of one of the twins, who had been missing since the night of the murder.

Krissi never paid much attention to the news even if it was all Sam would watch on TV. She found it depressing; hearing about the awful things that happened, told to you in a calm and detached way, knowing you were powerless to be able to reach out and tweak the world for the better... Of course, her ladies had given her the information, but that was not the same as seeing names and faces on a screen, frozen forever in a past that could never be reclaimed because now Death barred the door.

In the comments sections of the various news sites she trawled and on social media, when she went searching for the profiles of her long-ago friends, she was able to piece together the general consensus. It was a mixture comprised of five percent known facts, fifteen percent intelligent guesswork, and eighty percent random conjecture, slurs, and gossip. The school day link between the twins and Celina was well-known, and when you added the absent girlfriend, the end result was a story that suggested a jealous and jilted lover turned murderess. The more lurid versions of this story suggested that the brother's swapped identities frequently in order to swap partners, in order to increase the amount of nookie they were conning out of the two women.

Krissi was close to fooling herself into accepting this version of reality when Tony Peacock was killed. On his birthday.

In a hardcore gay fetish club.

This last detail was very hard for the online community to fold into any existing scenario that had evolved to explain away the tragedies.

She came very close to going to the police.

But...

But the story was still insane, no matter how you looked at it.

A lollipop man had come back from the dead to murder the Skeleton Gang one by one?

Wasting police time was a serious offence...

But she had evidence! Random photos from some anonymous creep on the Web! Ghosts could use social media too!

...and what were you doing on the nights of each of the deaths?

It was not that she was worried about being implicated in the deaths, far from it, but more that she knew that time was against her... if the insane belief that Adele had proposed were true, however incredibly unlikely it might be... then Krissi was guessing that the few days she had to go before it was her own 21st were simply not enough to convince any members of Her Majesty's constabulary to get an exorcist involved.

Krissi made a plan.

First, she had to get Sam somewhere safe before her birthday.

She had no choice. She'd have to leave him with her mum.

*****

Her mum had stopped drinking after the phone call, but she still smelled like she'd explode if you lit a match too close to her.

The main stipulation Krissi had given her mum whenever she allowed the older woman to look after Sam, was strictly no drinking when he was around. And she'd been as good as her word. She hadn't been expecting Sam today, of course, which excused her.

But Krissi had never trusted her to go a whole night without getting pissed.

"Sammy!" she screeched upon opening the door. "My best boy! Give your nan a kiss an' a cuddle!"

Sam grinned at the older woman. She wasn't swaying, but her eyes were having trouble focusing on him, and he thought that was funny. When he dashed into her arms for the promised cuddle, that was when she swayed backwards, but she didn't stagger, and she didn't fall. She crouched so that the boy could bury his head in her shoulder.

"And how is my best boy? He's going to stay with his old nan for a few days isn't he? Does Sammy love his nanny?"

Sam's head nodded against her shoulder, and Krissi felt a flare of jealous hate bloom in her gut.

Ridiculous, he only sees her at Christmas and his birthdays and a handful of other times a year, how the frig... No. No, this isn't the time.

She had a brief moment of vertigo as she looked at the older woman framed by the dimly lit corridor of her childhood. Down there, to the right, was her old bedroom. Down there, to the left, was the combined kitchen and living room. At the end of the corridor, her mum's room with the en suite bathroom which had to do for both of them. The interior of the maisonette hadn't been decorated in Krissi's lifetime; there were dirty smudges on the wallpaper, and stains in the greasy carpet, whose origins she could remember.

"Hi Debbie," said Krissi.

Her mum looked up from the cuddle she shared with Sam.

"I'm your mum, so call me it," she said.

"I'm not having this argument again, not here, not now," said Krissi.

Sam's head, buried in her shoulder, turned so that he could whisper something in her ear.

"Wassat Sammy? Oh. Right, right, right, okay, I won't."

Krissi's mum gently disentangled herself from Sam. When she straightened up she had to brace herself on the door frame. Flakes of paint crumbled from it.

"Come in, then, both of you," she said, gesturing as she turned and made her way down the corridor that was frozen in time.

Sam trotted after her eagerly whilst Krissi shouldered the rucksack she had hastily stuffed with a week's worth of his clothes.

If the corridor was a decaying museum, the living room and kitchen were preserved in aspic. Nothing was different except for new patches of stains on the ground from spilled food. The single sofa sagged with the weight of its years, and on the right hand cushion sat a lap tray with a plate of food.

Fish fingers. Chips. Peas. All overcooked; the fish would be dry even under a thick layer of ketchup, the ends of the oven chips were blackened like spent matches, and the peas were wrinkly as fingertips after a bath.

Frig me...

"When your mum said you were coming to stay I made your favourite dinner to celebrate."

Krissi almost lost it there and then, but Sam seemed happy enough. He hopped onto the sofa and his grandmother grandly presented him the plate of food which Krissi had eaten almost every night of her childhood.

She never served him crap like that, so here it was a treat.

She glanced towards the kitchen area, divided from the living part of the room by a counter that also served as a breakfast bar. The glass plastic recycling tub on the floor next to the fridge. It was full of bottles, bottles who shared a label as familiar to Krissi as her own reflection.

"Do you want your nan to put the telly on for you Sammy?" her mother asked.

Sam nodded.

Then he said;

"The news, please."

Krissi's mum looked at her.

Krissi shrugged.

"It's all he watches these days," she said.

Her mum put the news channel on and then, in the exaggerated way the half-cut think is the height of subtlety, beckoned Krissi out of the room into the corridor, closing the door after her.

"So," she said. Though she was still lit, her tone and demeanour changed from lovely goofy nanny, to the woman Krissi remembered much more. "What the fuck is going on? Why does my darling daughter who barely acknowledges me most of the year suddenly decide that her mum, who's the fucking devil on earth or something, who raised her single-handed somehow, but y'know, let's call me Debbie, I can go fuck myself..."

She stopped talking, realising she was rambling.

"So," she said again, her bloodshot eyes holding Krissi's. "Why are you suddenly entrusting your 'drunk cunt' of a mother, as you put it so memorably once, with her own grandson?"

"It's complicated," said Krissi. "Look, it doesn't really matter, does it? You're always asking for more time with Sam, so here you go. Frig, let's call it a test drive; look after him for the next few days, stay dry, and maybe we'll make this a regular thing. You would like that, wouldn't you?"

Krissi could see that her mother wanted to argue the toss -she was an alcoholic, not stupid; she knew there was a lot more going on- but she also truly did want to see more of her grandson, so now her mind began to work the issue over.

Eventually she said, "Regular? Like, once a month, nanny and Sammy time, yeah?"

"If you stay dry," said Krissi.

The chronic drunk, confronted with an ultimatum in which the drink features as a yes or no deal, can't help but pause to think about it. Anyone else would have said yes, of course I'm choosing blood over booze... but that pause reminded Krissi why she didn't want to do this.

"Sure, no problem, I can knock it on the head for a few days," said her mum. "No problem. Easy. Easy."

Krissi hated herself, but... she had no choice. Sam couldn't be around her; something terrible was happening to the Skeleton Gang, and she'd never put him in harm's way.

She pressed thirty quid into her mum's hand.

"Buy him decent food," she said. "And keep the receipts, I want to see that money go on something other than fish frigging fingers."

"Of course!"

Krissi held her finger up.

"I mean it Debbie; no booze, no frigging fish fingers."

Her mum held her hands up, rolling her eyes.

"I heard you the first fucking time."

Krissi went and said goodbye to Sam.

She'd imagined that this new situation would have upset him; he'd never spent time apart from her overnight before. But he seemed happy enough, eating overcooked chips and watching the news.

Somehow, she managed to get out of the room without crying.

She was terrified. She felt sick. She couldn't...

But then as she was leaving the corridor, stepping out the front door and trying not to let herself think, a thought occurred to her that she realised she really should have had before. It was a question, and even as it entered her head she nearly dismissed it, because after all, how much of her childhood would her mum even recall if she had given a toss about it at the time, let alone pickled her brain in cheap vodka?

But still.

"Debbie, do you remember when I was little, when I went to St Edwards?" she asked.

Her mum stood framed by the faded and aged corridor.

"Of course I do," she said. "You used to take yourself off on your own every morning, right little madam you were."

Krissi bit down on a response she wanted to make, the observation that she had to take herself off as her mother refused to leave the pit of her bed until midday.

"Do you remember about the lollipop man who killed himself?"

Her mum stared blearily at her, apparently not remembering anything of the sort.

Should have expected it...

But her mum wasn't confused because she didn't recall the tragedy.

"The lollipop man?" she said. "I remember Mr Lucky Fucker, yeah, but I don't think he topped himself. Who would, if they had his kind of fucking cash?"

NINE

THE GLASS of vodka shook as she held it in both hands and guided it towards her mouth.

Krissi watched, her emotions in a whirl, her mind spinning as well, but feeling as if the spin were counter-wise to the whirl She felt dizzy and wrenched and somehow also coldly lucid.

Adele drank the drink quickly. The ice cube's rattled.

Krissi was hoping the booze would calm her, acting as a kind of brief substitute for whatever it was her body actually craved.

They sat in the cold beer garden alone, a garden in name only, a yard behind the pub for smokers to get their fix. A crisp packet scraped across the broken concrete, dandelions growing up through the cracks.

"So you believe me now, yeah? Because of Tony?"

"I don't know what I believe," said Krissi. "Half of the Skeleton Gang are dead. That's all I really know, but I don't believe anything."

Adele sniggered, staring down at the ground between her feet.

"It was Mr Bartleby," she said. "You'll believe that when he comes for you."

"Adele..."

"We killed him. As good as. And now he's killing us."

"...he isn't dead."

Adele looked up sharply.

"At least, I don't think he is," said Krissi.

Adele just stared at her. She had stopped shivering and shaking.

Krissi continued.

"My mum told me the story, or at least, what she remembered. It was massive news at the time; Mr Bartleby was a volunteer lollipop man. It wasn't his job, because he didn't need a job. He won the lottery when he was twenty-one, from a ticket his mum bought him as a birthday present. He was a mummy's boy apparently, still lived with her, and when he won he bought their council house and then... well, apparently he had no imagination because he didn't really do anything with the rest of his winnings. He volunteered as a lollipop man just to have something to do."

Adele was staring at the ground again.

"Debbie... my mum doesn't think he killed himself. Apparently he just stopped coming to work, and nobody saw him again. No-one really knew what happened. He definitely didn't step in front of a lorry."

"But, that's what people said in school."

Krissi shrugged.

"You know what kids are like; they make stuff up. Probably what happened is Mr Bartleby just got frigged off with... well, me, slagging him off all the time, and seeing as though he didn't need to work he just said, sod it. I know I would."

Adele was frowning.

"Have you been to the police?" she asked.

"No. I mean, this is stuff I just found out two hours ago. I thought about going to them before, but what was I going to say? Was I going to tell them that a dead lollipop man was killing my old school friends because we used to call him names? That would be..."

"...it sounds like the sort of crazy shit a fucking junkie would come up with right?" said Adele with a bitter smile.

Krissi said nothing.

"It is, isn't it? Why do you think I never went to them, when I figured that was what was going on? That was why I had to contact you, I thought maybe if you were convinced, you were more likely to be listened to. You've got your shit together, and I'm a fucking druggie."

Krissi reached out and took one of Adele's hands. It was so thin, so cold.

Adele looked astonished.

"I'm sorry," said Krissi, and hoped her old friend would understand what she was saying sorry for. "But now, well, it looks like he's probably still alive. So... you know, it could be him who killed Celina and Tony and Cliff and Duane... it's still crazy, I mean, I don't know why he would, it can't just be because we were horrible to him when we were kids... but if he is alive, then he would be a suspect, right? So now we can go to the police, and at least they wouldn't think we were frigging barking...."

"No!"

Adele's outburst startled Krissi. She stared at the other woman, who looked completely panicked. She was watching as Adele blinked her eyes furiously, then seemed to try and rally herself.

"No, we can't, I mean. Not yet. I mean, what have we got for them at the moment? Just an idea, and it's an idea I had when I thought that it was, like, some sort of fucking spook doing the murdrers! We should go to the police, but we're going to need something a bit more, right?"

Krissi was doubtful.

"There's the pictures he sent me... did he send them to you too?"

Adele looked blank for a moment, then she nodded vigorously.

"Oh yeah, I meant those too, but I meant maybe we could..." she paused, and licked her lips. "We could go to his house."

The words were so astonishing that for a moment, Krissi couldn't think.

"What do you mean, go to his house?" she asked.

"His house! You said, he bought his mum's house right? Don't we know where that is? We were going to go and egg it on Halloween weren't we..."

Krissi was nodding. She did have a memory of that. She had sent the twins to follow him home once, hadn't she? And they had found out where he lived. Yes... they had been planning on egging the place at Halloween; she had planned it like a military operation, buying a a carton of eggs every weekend for about two months before hand because the shops wouldn't let you buy loads to close to the night...

"I can't remember where it is," said Krissi. "He disappeared long before Halloween, so I never got the twins to take us there for a reccy."

"I remember," said Adele. "Cliff told me. I know exactly where his house is."

"And you think we should go there... why? Shouldn't we just tell the police?"

Adele was standing up, and shaking her head.

"No, no, no, we can't, because what if he isn't there, what if he sold the place and it's just some family living there now? If we sent the filth around and we didn't have that bit right, they won't even think of investigating further... and we already know he's the one doing the killing! All we need to do is go to the street, get a look at the house, see what the situation is... and then we can take it from there."

"I don't know..." said Krissi.

"You said your Sam is with your mum, so you know he's safe for the moment, right? And how many days is it 'til your birthday?"

"The weekend, I told you. Saturday. Two days."

"So we don't have time to fuck about. We need to get all our facts right, then go to the coppers and let them nail the bastard in one swoop. You know, like a raid."

Krissi was starting to see the vague sense of what Adele was saying. At the moment they had their belief that they knew who murdered their old friends, and whilst it sounded far-fetched, it was possible. And she did have those photos of the hedgehog cakes, sent by the Scrivener... she could tell them about that Moby Dick story, let them see the connection.

And maybe Mr Bartleby was at that house. It wasn't impossible. If her mum was right, he'd bought the place because it was his family home; after he moved away he could have kept it, because with his lottery money he wouldn't have had to sell it, would he?

She wasn't sure... but her birthday was two days away.

Reluctantly, she asked Adele when they should go around and have a look.

Adele said, "Why not right now? Do you have a car?"

"No, there's no point having one around my way."

"Even better. It's only over on the other side of the river, only one bus away."

As they left the pub and headed for the nearest bus stop, Krissi briefly wondered what those two words meant; "even better". But things were moving so quickly that she couldn't concentrate on puzzling out their meaning.

The next few days would have been very different if she had.

TEN

"...GOING TO die here."

There had been more words before this, but they had been a mumbled blur in the same way that her surroundings had just been a smear of colours and vague outlines. As her vision had sharpened and she had begun to make out details of her surroundings, so had the blundering nonsense sounds gradually resolved into syllables and sense.

Her other senses came back to her, also seeming to come into focus.

She could smell shit.

She could taste blood.

She felt awful. All-day hangover awful.

The sunflowers grew from left to right.

She was lying on her side, looking at old wallpaper.

She was on some kind of thin mattress, no sheet, laid on the floor.

Her head throbbed in sick-time with her pulse, an ache that seemed to beat outward from the very middle of her brain as if it contained a tiny, agonised heart at its centre.

Gingerly, she pushed herself up until she was reclining on one elbow, and had a better look around the room. At the moment she had no real thoughts beyond the pain, and was only mechanically going through the motions.

The whole room was decorated with the peeling, sunflower patterned wallpaper. It was empty apart from a bucket in one corner, a second thin, stained mattress, and the young woman who was sat on it, emaciated legs drawn up with her skinny arms hugging them, looking at Krissi over the tops of her bony knees. Her eyes were raw and hollow with deep purple circles under them, and her hair was a matted thatch.

The young woman lifted her head enough for her mouth to be visible. Her lips were cracked and crusted with dry blood.

"We're both going to die here," she repeated.

*****

The girl's name was Nadia. She was Cliff's missing girlfriend. She had been abducted by the lollipop man.

She had spent the past three months locked in this room. She hadn't known that she had been there for three months, because she had no way of knowing how much time had elapsed. When Krissi told her the date, Nadia had screamed.

The girl was emaciated because her captors barely fed her.

"Captors... You mean, there's more than just... him?" asked Krissi.

Nadia nodded.

"Yesh, there'sh two, the lollipop man and thish woman.Mosht of the time itsh her that comesh in, bringsh food and water and takesh my bucket away."

The bucket in the corner was the source of the stench of shit. It was what Nadia had for a toilet.

"They feed me rubbish, left over scrapsh, like pizza crustsh, or peelingsh; one week, I think all I had was black banana skinsh."

When she spoke, it sounded like her mouth was full of spit, making her speech mushy.

She didn't resist, because she couldn't. Her wrists were bound with cable ties, and her legs were bound with ties around her knees. Where the cables were tied they had cut into her flesh, which was raw, oozing with pus. She could stand if she shuffled to one wall and levered herself up it, could stand to go and squat over the bucket, but mostly she crawled. Her food and water were served in dog bowls.

"It took a long time to get my balance right. I can get around by shuffling. But it'sh tiring so I only do it so that I don't shit or pissh all over the floor. I'm not an animal."

"But your wrists," said Krissi. "Why don't you chew through the ties at your wrists?"

"I tried that, said Nadia. "He wasn't happy when he found me."

She opened her mouth.

All the teeth in the left side of her face, from her canines to her molars, were gone. It had happened some time ago, as her gums had healed into an angry looking mass like wads of chewed up bubble gum.

"He shtomped on my face until they all came out."

"But then, why aren't I tied up?"Krissi asked.

Nadia shrugged.

"I wouldn't like to wonder," she said.

The lollipop man never abused her, at least, not since he had kicked most of her teeth out. There was no sex stuff.

The woman had fingered her a few times though. Fingered Nadia whilst she masturbated.

The first time was right after the face-stomping, when Nadia had been too dazed too do anything, and after that she had pretty much resigned herself to dying in that room. She ate the waste food, drank the water, and continued to void herself in a bucket after struggling to her feet and hobbling her way over to it, purely as a mechanical response.

At first, Krissi had reached for Nadia, intending to free her of the cable ties that cruelly cut into her wrists and around the tops of her calves, but the other woman had shrunk from her, the memory of her beating making her resist until finally she had screamed at Krissi to leave her alone. After that, Krissi had got up and paced around the room, looking more closely at what was to be seen.

The bucket hadn't been emptied in days. The colours and textures of what was festering in their made her stomach flop over greasily, threatening puke.

She tried the door. It had an old fashioned knob with an old fashioned keyhole. It was locked.

She went to where the window was. The boards nailed over it allowed in the light, but dimly, as if it were twilight outside. The boards were all firm, despite the thumb wide gaps between them through which illumination reached. There was netting over the windows, preventing her from getting an idea on what it looked out onto.

Nadia had told Krissi how she had ended up in the room, every humiliating detail; her three way with the brothers which was interrupted by Death thundering into the flat. She described what became of Cliff and Duane in a cold, matter-of-fact way... including to when the lollipop man had come into the room, placed his boot on Cliff's left buttock, and pulled his stick out with a long, wet, slick sound.

"Then he smacked me over the head with it, again," she said. "That'sh how he knocked me out the first time. Like something out of a cartoon. And when I woke up I started my new life in here. Eating rotting garbage, shitting in a bucket, and letting some junkie whore wank herself off as she sticksh most of her fisht into me."

Krissi said nothing. What could she have said? The entire thing was so nightmarish; she was having trouble believing it was real.

Whenever she had bad dreams, she often became aware of the fact that she was dreaming, and when she did she urged herself to wake up, tried to force herself out of them. In those dreams, the act of waking up felt like a huge "blink"sensation in her mind, something she could make happen if she tried hard enough. So convinced was she that this was not happening, she found herself trying to "blink" with her mind... but of course, no matter how hard she tried to force the sensation, to jolt herself out of the nightmare, it wouldn't happen.

This was real.

"Sho?"

Krissi snapped back to the present, the awful truth that she was awake and this was happening.

"So?" she repeated.

"Sho how did you end up here?" Nadia asked.

Krissi laughed, a weird, bubbly pop of pure hysteria.

"That junkie you mentioned," she said. "She's an old friend. She brought me here."

*****

The house looked little different from every other in the terrace in which it formed the third but last home. Maybe it was more run down than the others, but apart from that, Krissi couldn't understand why someone who had won so much money would have bought it, not when there were so much nicer places even in the same area of town.

The front yard was barely big enough to park a scooter, if you could squeeze it through the gate, but held only grey gravel. The windows were smeary, and the drawn curtains beyond were heavy, dark drapes that obscured any light that might have been on inside.

They were across the road, a few houses down, trying to be inconspicuous. Both sides of the road were jammed tight with parked cars and vans.

"Are you sure that's the house?"Krissi asked again.

"Yes, I told you, yes!" said Adele.

"It doesn't look like anyone's there."

"Well, there's no way of telling, is there? Not without going over and knocking."

"We aren't doing that."

Adele thought, chewing her thumbnail. Then she had an idea.

"Round the back! There's alleys that run up the back of these houses, we can go around the back and see what can be seen!"

Krissi agreed reluctantly, still believing this was a fool's errand.

They had gone the long way around, Adele counting off the back gates of tiny gardens until they reached the one she believed had to be it.

"So, now what?" asked Krissi.

Adele tried the gate. It was unlocked. She pushed it open.

The back garden was overgrown, a thick jungle of brambles and nettles, with colour added by a huge fox glove flower that was growing out of the drum of a rusting tumble-dryer thrown in one corner.

Adele began to move forward. Krissi gripped her arm, and held on even when she felt physical revulsion at how thin the woman's bicep was under her cheap jacket.

"You can't be serious! We aren't going in!"

Adele wrenched free.

"There's someone home!" she said. "Look, there's a bit of light at the window!"

There was indeed light, but it looked wrong. It was the kind of strip of light you expect to see if the curtains weren't fully drawn, but there was more than one long thin sliver, as if the curtains beyond the grimy windows had been slashed repeatedly.

"We'll just peek in, just a quick peek."

"Adele no..."

But she was already moving quietly up the broken concrete path that lead through the wildly overgrown garden, a path that lead to the window with its slivers of light, and a backdoor with peeling pink paintwork.

Krissi, dread gripping her stomach in a huge, cold hand that had too many fingers, said "frig it" under her breath and paced after her.

At the window, Adele was cupping her hands around her eyes as if miming she had binoculars and was squinting at one sliver of light.

"What do you see?"

Adele shrugged.

"Can't really tell, the gap is a bit too small..."

Krissi got up close to the glass and imitated her friend, looking in at a different strip of illumination.

It really was difficult to be certain what was inside the room. But then, in the dimness, Krissi wasn't certain if she were even looking through tatty curtains. Whatever the obscured material was beyond the windowsill, it looked oddly firm. It was as she tried to understand what she was looking at that she heard the squeal of a handle being turned, and the whine of hinges flexing as the back door was opened.

Krissi's heart trilled and her stomach dropped.

She turned to look at Adele.

Adele was already half inside the house.

She'd tried the door, and found it unlocked, heading inside, not someone inside coming out.

"Adele!" hissed Krissi.

Her old friend ignored her, vanishing into the gloomy interior of the building.

There was an agonised internal debate on Krissi's part, and she whisper-hissed Adele's name a half dozen more times before she gingerly approached the open portal.

A faint smell drifted from the inside of the house. It was sweet and rotten, and under that sweet rottenness there was something else... The backdoor opened into a kitchen.

"Adele..." she whispered into the shadows of the house. The only relief from the murk was a thin line of light on the ground about six feet inside, on the right. The door to the room with the light, that light slipping under it. That light illuminated some kind of mess on the floor, something sticky and textured like vomit.

"Naughty hedgehog."

In her surprise, at first she thought it was the voice of the woman she had followed this far on a foolish mission. But it wasn't, she realised, as the owner of the voice seemed to unfold from the darkest corner of the kitchen and rushed at her.

Then there was pain and the darkness seeped into everything.

*****

The slivers of light had been the gaps between the boards over the window. Krissi touched the boards with her fingertips, realising that not so long before, she had been on the other side of them. It was a gap of feet, but it might as well have been miles.

Hours had passed. She had told Nadia everything she knew, both facts and conjecture.

The other woman had listened numbly.

When Krissi had finished, Nadia had made a strange, strangled noise that could have been laughter.

"Sho this guy is shum bloke you upset when you were a kid, and now he'sh come to kill your friendsh all these yearsh later? That is a sheriously crazy grudge to bear. And what doesh that make me?"

Krissi considered.

"After I started taking it seriously, I read as much about the murders as I could. You're the only missing person; the others were gotten whilst they were alone. I think you got in the way, but I don't know why he didn't just kill you. That would have made more sense."

Nadia looked at Krissi.

"Why he didn't just kill me..." she echoed. "It would have made more shenshe... I know I'm a bit fucked up at the moment, but that wash cold."

"Yes Christine, that was a highly insensitive way of putting it. But I had my reasons."

The voice was muffled by the door it had come from behind.

Nadia moaned. It was a low, dismal sound, the sound of an animal, of something that had given in to despair.

"It'sh him..." she whispered.

The lock disengaged with a smooth click.

ELEVEN

MR BARTLEBY the lollipop man was in full uniform, stick grasped in one hand, the other hand hidden behind his back.

For just a moment when the door had opened and framed him, Krissi had seen him as he once had been, an adult, a giant, towering over her, a part of a mystifying world which she did not understand, a world which was both baffling and cruel, which made her attack it in self-defence.

But he was no giant.

Mr Bartleby just looked like any middle aged man in a hi-vis trench coat and billed cap, the kind of man who volunteered not only to help keep school children safe on their way to school, but also pitched in at every school fete, setting up tables and selling raffle tickets. He was smooth shaven with cropped grey hair, his skin was tanned and he had weak brown eyes.

He looked like anybody at all.

He was grinning. His teeth were his single most remarkable feature; they were absolutely perfect in shape and spacing, and flawlessly white. In such an average face, they looked out of place, like they were too large for his head.

That, and his uniform was filthy.

The filth was dried blood and flecks of tissue, stains won from the insides of other humans. Wrapped around the shaft of the lollipop was something that looked like a skinned snake.

But worst of all, even after ten years and all the recent turbulence of horror, he was recognisably the same man she had said such awful things to, and about, when she was a tearaway child.

"Look at you!" he said, his voice slightly croaky, but full of mocking humour. "The naughtiest little hedgehog, all grown up... but not too much, eh? Lack of basic nutrition at the key developmental stages has left you a half-pint for life, hasn't it?"

Nadia whimpered.

Krissi was rooted to the spot.

"But it's nice to see that you've learnt, learnt by bad example," he continued. "You serve up decent plates of grub, and that boy of yours is growing up big and strong, ain't he?"

Krissi said nothing, but something in her mind lit up. Instinct. Primal.

"...and he's quite the little artist too."

"Don't you say another fucking word," she hissed.

His eyes widened, and so did his grin.

"Oh, oh, oh, yes! Mumma hedgehog has claws! Mumma hedgehog doesn't like me talking about her little hoglet!"

He was fast.

In two swift movements, he brought the end of the lollipop pole up from the ground and whipped it across the side of her face with a loud *crack!* It was like being smashed in the side of the head with a broom handle, but he'd only done it to startle her, to leave her defence open as he kicked her hard in the stomach, winding her and knocking her backwards, making her trip over her own feet.

When she hit the ground her guts rebelled, and even though they were in agony they convulsed and she puked on the floor.

Nadia screamed.

That was when he stomped on the side of Krissi's head, bouncing her skull off the vomit slick floorboards.

She lay there, stunned, unable to process what had just happened.

Nadia was sobbing, terrified that he was coming for her. But he wasn't.

Mr Bartleby only had eyes for Krissi.

He crouched down next to her, using his stick for support.

He held out a hand, palm down, indicating height.

"I remember when you were like this, knee-high to a high-knee as my mum would have put it. Such a tiny little thing, and yet I used to dread that moment every day when you and your motley crew would show up. You were always such a clever little cunt, waiting until there was no parents or other kids around... nobody to hear the things you used to say to me."

Krissi eyes were full of tears and she was gasping for breath through a mouth and throat still slick with caustic bile.

"Those thing you used to say to me...." he made *tsk, tsk* noises, shaking his head. But his grin had not wavered once. "I'd been doing the job for a few years, and I thought I'd gotten used to the rotten little hedgehogs who turned up every year, those lovely little kiddies who were just turning into sour little shits and off to secondary school. All the names they used on me, kicking out against a soft target, an authority figure who could never fight back... But then you came along."

Krissi managed to get her breathing under control, but the blazing pain in her stomach and her head were making it impossible for her to marshal sense from what he was saying. The meaning was arriving long seconds after the words.

"*Peeee-doooooo*," said Mr Bartleby in as high-pitch a voice as he could make. "You remember? You used to call me a pervert, a kiddy fiddler. You'd say stuff like, like, you knew I was thinking about sticking my cock up your hairless cunt..."

His head was shaking again.

"Two things about that; first, I couldn't figure out where you got the language from."

He sighed.

"The second thing was... I didn't know how you were able to read my fucking mind."

He stood up and began to pace the room, his steps measured and sure, his lollipop held like a shepherd would hold his staff, both used to usher the innocent from danger.

"I'd always had these feelings, but I knew they were wrong. My mum told me so. The rest of society told me so. So I kept those feelings to myself, and never did anything. And then, twist of fate, the lottery ticket my mum brought for my twenty-first birthday, just so happened to be the winner. Jackpot! It was a double roll-over, seventeen point three million quid! Set for life! But there was a problem...

"I was set for life, yeah, but even before the money I had no idea what I wanted to do with my life. No real interests or ambitions. I liked footy, but I wasn't much cop at a kick-about, and that's not something you can buy, is it, skill? I bought my mum's house for her, and in return, that beautiful woman who had given me life and raised me and loved me, and then won me a fortune, she did the greatest thing anyone has ever done for me; she gave me the advice that I should do some good, even if only in the local community. I ought to give back. Now, my mum was a wise old woman, and I could see that she was right... but still, I had no idea about exactly what I could do to give back...

"I got the idea for being a lollipop man from this documentary about Ghandi."

Krissi was able to breath properly again, and was making more and more sense of what the bastard was saying, but then, when he mentioned the Indian pacifist, she looked straight at Mr Bartleby.

He saw her looking.

Gently, very gently, he placed the filth-caked sole of his boot against the side of her face and pushed her back down into her vomit.

Krissi smelt sweetness, and something brown and soft was smeared across her cheek.

She struggled to free herself, but he was too strong. He pinned her head to the ground whilst her stomach pulsed with waves of pain, a sensation like something vital within her insides had been torn.

"Ghandi would take girls into his bed at night," said the lollipop man. "Six, seven year old girls. He was testing himself, to see if he could resist temptation. I suppose it's a bit like an alcoholic going into a bar and ordering lemonade, just to prove to himself that he doesn't have a problem. I have to admit, that's why I wanted to be around kids. To prove to myself that I wasn't what I was. So, I'd be helping out, giving back, being a good bloke... and I'd know that I was a good bloke, because not only was I giving freely of my time, but I'd be proving to myself and God that just because I thought about children, it didn't mean I was ever going to do anything."

The boot came off her cheek, and she recognised what the stuff on the sole had been; cake.

"Until you came along, and saw right through me."

"...fuck you," whispered Krissi.

He looked down at her, startled.

"Hmm? You want me to fuck you? Oh, once upon a time I'd have jumped at the chance, but you're a bit long in the tooth and loose in the gash for me now!"

He paused.

"Sammy, on the other hand..."

*****

She wanted a drink. She couldn't have a drink. If she had a drink, she couldn't have Sam over again. She couldn't have a drink.

She wanted a drink.

Around and around went her thoughts.

They had watched the news until it had depressed her too much, and after wracking her brain for an activity for them to do she had a great idea. She knew how much he liked to draw, so she had introduced him to a drawing game that he hadn't heard about before.

"Well, normally you need three people, but we can do it with just us two. What you do is, the first person draws the top bit, we're drawing a person, so the first person draws the head, and then folds the paper over to hide what they did except for the very edge, so that there are a few lines for the next person to draw the body, right? And then when they've drawn the body, they fold the picture again, leaving a little bit exposed again, and the last person draws the legs... and then at the end you unfold it and you see what you all drew!"

Sam thought about this.

"It sounds fun. Can we play?" he asked.

She fetched a takeaway menu for the Canton House and a couple of pens, two Biros. One was chewed, and the other had a crack running the length of the barrel. She unfolded the menu on the lap-tray Sam had eaten his tea off.

"Look, we can use the blank space at the bottom of this menu, it's already folded into threes for us... OK Sammy, you're the artist, you can start."

It was as Sam carefully and secretively began drawing the head that she wished she had a drink. Her buzz was wearing off.

You can't have a drink, not with Sam here. Not tonight, at all, in case he wakes up. Kids do that, get nightmares and wake up and need to be cuddled, and you can't do that if your pissed on the sofa...

She wasn't going to be able to do this. And if that was true, why, didn't it mean that every horrible thing her daughter had ever said about her was true as well? Her ego felt threatened.

After what seemed like half an hour but was actually a third of that time, Sam was satisfied with what he had done. He folded the first third of the menu over, and then pushed it back on itself enough to reveal the tail ends of pen-strokes.

"Your turn, nanny," he said.

At the word "nanny" she suddenly thought that actually, maybe she could get through the night without another drink.

She accepted the lap-tray with the menu lying on it, and spent nearly a minute trying to think what to draw.

What would be funny?

Ah.

Muscle men were funny. Huge biceps, big broad pecs, a six-pack... She started to draw.

Sam tried to peek.

"Oi! Nosey-parker!"

He grinned, and covered his eyes with both hands with a great dramatic flourish.

When she was done, she felt quite pleased. Her bulging, idiot muscle-man body wasn't bad. Maybe she had a talent for drawing as well? Maybe it skipped a generation, like diabetes.

She folded over what she had done, careful to leave a tiny bit showing so Sam had a place to start the last bit, the legs.

It was as Sam set to the task with full concentration, head close to the paper, tilted to one side, with his free arm curled protectively around, that the doorbell rang.

It was a bit late for visitors, not that she got any, generally. In fact, the last time anyone had rung was a pair of boys in suits with name tags, who turned out to be American Mormon missionaries... she'd been half-cut at the time, and had exploded with religious fury, telling them she was C of E and they could tell the Pope to fuck off.

Not that she had been in a church in years...

Whilst she went to see who was at the door, Sam drew.

The drawing game had a name; it was called "The Exquisite Corpse." The Corpse that Sam and his grandmother had worked on would later become just another piece of evidence, and normally would have ended up in storage, sealed away along with so many other pieces of paper that were connected to dreadful crimes. But the Corpse had a second life, thanks to pictures taken surreptitiously on phones by coppers and court clerks, and it became in its own way as famous as the clown paintings of the American serial killer John Wayne Gacey.

The heavily muscled torso should have been out of place thanks to the less skilful technique of its execution, but somehow it was not.

Atop the broad shoulders was a face recognisable to generations of children. Who else could have such a huge, hooked nose, and upturned, jutting chin that made them look like a caricature of the crescent moon, than Mr Punch? In addition, the Corpse had no legs as such; the torso extended into a fluted shape that faded into the long face and snout of an animal, and if there was any doubt about which animal it was supposed to be, the child artist had added a tongue lapping up tiny black ants.

TWELVE

"PAEDOPHILE'S PARADISE, that's what they should call the Philippines. Actually, all of south-east Asia is like a sweet shop for pre-pube boy pussy."

That was where Mr Bartleby had been for the past decade, he told his audience, an audience of two women, one emaciated and terrified, the other growing more and more furious. His wealth had bought him the ability to do almost anything he had wanted, and so he had bought a small compound for himself in a village outside Manilla, staffed it with scum who'd do anything for money, and begun a ten year reign of depravity.

"I say pussy, but actually, boys or girls, it didn't matter. Any hole is a goal."

In a country where poverty is the norm, the rich can do as they want.

"I made connections, mainly re-selling. Bad blokes. Just because you personally might think last year's model isn't cute anymore, or has gotten a bit loose, you'd be amazed how many bad blokes with a smaller budget don't mind sloppy seconds. Like my mate Blue, right, one time he... Actually, I'll tell you about that a bit later."

Indonesia, Thailand, Vietnam, Cambodia, Laos...

"Thanks to those connections, I was able to purchase from further afield as well. Now, I don't care how politically correct anybody reckons they are, we're all a bit racist when you get right down to it, and I was missing dipping my wick in my own gene pool..."

Krissi was aware of her heart, her blood rushing in her ears and a sensation like cold inferno roaring in her. She could never have believed herself capable of the rage inside she felt.

The lollipop man saw it written on her face, and it was enough to bring him back to the present, out of fond memories filled with screams.

"Now, now, mumma hedgehog, I might be a bad bloke, but I'm not the worse. Some blokes I've met out there, they really wreck 'em..." He shuddered. "And eat the evidence."

"If you lay one finger on my son..."

"You'll what? Kill me? Ain't going to happen, Christine. This is the real world."

She found herself on her hands and knees, crouching, coiling, ready to leap at him.

He reached inside his hi-vis trench coat and pulled out a gun.

"Don't be silly. If you're silly, I'll blow off your kneecaps and elbows, then put a bullet in both your ankles. The bad bloke who taught me that little trick, my mate Blue, calls it a six-pack. You'll only be able to watch after that."

Krissi stayed where she was, although for a moment she saw herself, in her mind's eye, springing on the lunatic bastard, swatting the dull grey gun to one side and then pushing her thumbs deep into his eyes before she started tearing at his face.

He watched her and she watched him, until both understood what was going to happen.

Nadia moaned.

"What about me?" she demanded. "What do I have to do with any of this? Let me go, please, I promise I won't say anything."

Mr Bartleby frowned.

"Oh, you were just unfortunate, wrong place, wrong time," he said. "But thanks to you, I've learned a little bit more about lairage."

Nadia, pressed against the wall, echoed that word with a question in her voice.

"Lairage?"

"Farming term. It's to do with how long you can leave off feeding and watering livestock before slaughter, before significant weight loss sets in," said the lollipop man. "Research for a connection of mine, he's a bit tight-fisted you see. Doesn't want to waste money feeding any of his stable who are, well, who are off to join the Lost-Boys, if you get me."

He turned the gun on Nadia and shot her twice in the face.

Krissi couldn't even scream. The gun was deafening in the unfurnished room. Even Mr Bartleby was stunned, screwing his eyes closed, clenching his teeth and raising his laden hands to his ears.

She didn't think.

With reaction speed she never knew she had, with no conscious plan in her head, she was darting forward on all fours like an animal and launching herself at the lollipop man, her footsteps and hands slapping the bare boards inaudible thanks to the ringing in her ears.

She ploughed into his midriff. It wasn't a tackle, or any kind of attempt to bring him down, but just a sheer desire to hurt him, a clumsy attack born of fury and a desire to rip him to pieces if she could.

Both Krissi and the lollipop man hit the wall, her shoulder in his gut and head in his chest, screeching mindlessly.

She drove the wind out of him and they both tumbled to the ground. His stick fell to one side and the gun clattered to the ground.

Still stunned by the gunshots, and now struggling to breathe, Mr Bartleby wasn't able to protect his face as her hands turned into claws and she raked at his eyes and cheeks, still shrieking.

Her nails caught in his left eye and she pulled hard, ripping the bottom of his eyelid away.

He yelled, thrashed, and managed to backhand her across the jaw.

Krissi snarled, barely feeling the blow, and felt an intense wave of atavistic pleasure burst in her chest as her nails dug deep, raw, and bloody gouges all the way from his left temple to the corner of his mouth.

His hands found her face, smacked at her, slid down to grab her throat.

Still fighting on instinct, Krissi lunged at his face and bit his mouth, getting half of his lips and part of his chin between her teeth. Blood flooded over her tongue, and then she found herself shaking her head savagely side to side until twists of flesh came away.

Mr Bartleby screamed, and the sound penetrated the ringing in her ears and the joy of violence that was clouding her mind.

She found herself backing away, scuttling back off his hard, lean body wrapped in the stained hi-vis trench coat. She found herself on unsteady feet, looking at the whimpering figure she had created, astonished at her own capacity for destruction.

Mr Bartleby moaned and sobbed, a monster become a wretch.

In her head, the switch that had been set to FIGHT now flicked to FLIGHT.

Without questioning herself, Krissi made for the door, skirting the sobbing thing on the ground, half curled against the wall.

She almost passed the gun by.

Something told her not to.

She bent and scooped it up with a quick snatch, glancing at the lollipop man. But he was cradling his face, his sobs spiking every time his fingertips found fresh damage. The marks of her nails ran across his forehead and neck, his torn left eye leaked blood into his tears, and snot mixing with the spitty wound of his mouth.

The eye not obscured by blood suddenly glared from between his fingers.

"You fuggin bisshh!" he shouted through ruined lips. "You fuggin, fuggin BISSH!"

Krissi said nothing. She looked down at him and felt empty. The sheer adrenaline and violent fury of the past few minutes had been so intense, it was like they burnt out any emotion she should have been feeling. The weight of the gun in her hand suggested something to her, but a cold and logical part of her brain explained the simple truth; she was just an ordinary working mum, and all she knew about guns was what she had seen in films. The notion of cold-bloodedly pointing the thing at the wretch and pulling the trigger... in films, yes, but not real life. People like her didn't do things like that. She'd picked it up because it was common sense.

She had parts of Mr Bartleby's lips and flesh from his chin in her mouth.

She spat them on him.

Then, as if taking a football penalty, she kicked him in the side of the face. She felt her toes sink into his flesh, felt little snapping sensations as teeth were bent sideways and ripped from their gums.

"That was for her," she told him, meaning Nadia, and left the room.

Sam was at the front door.

The junkie was stood behind him, with a broken bottle pressed into the side of his throat.

A vodka bottle.

The brand her mum drank.

Sam was crying without sound, tears rolling down his cheeks as he shivered with fear, as quiet in terror as he was in happiness. He had wet himself, the tell-tale stain visible even in the dim light of the hallway.

Krissi had thought she was numb, and then she saw her son and her soul howled.

Something was ripped out of her hand

A cold ring of metal pressed into the side of her face.

A kiss from the gun he had reclaimed.

"Fuggin bissh," said Mr Bartleby.

THIRTEEN

IN THE middle of the table, the rotting hedgehog smiled idiotically, seeming to enjoy its decay.

Krissi held Sam's gaze. The boy was terrified, her son was scared out of his mind, and there was nothing she could do but stare at him and hope her eyes told him all the things she wanted him to know, all the beautiful lies he needed to hear;

That she wouldn't let anyone hurt him.

That everything was going to be okay.

That someone was going to save them.

The doorbell rang.

"Ahh!" said Mr Bartleby. "Dah birffdaa subba ish heah!"

Adele got up and went to answer the front door.

Krissi and Sam were seated at either end of the table, cable ties around their ankles and their wrists lashing them to the furniture. Mr Bartleby and the junkie had taken seats on the two long sides, and between the four of them the table had been laid for Krissi's "birthday supper."

The lollipop man had ordered in fish and chips. Or rather, Adele had; Mr Bartleby had tended his wounds as well as he was able with gauze and bandages and plasters, but the damage to his mouth meant he wasn't able to speak well enough to order a takeaway.

He had retreated upstairs to look after himself when Adele had successfully restrained both Krissi and Sam at gunpoint in the kitchen. After he had gone, the junkie began preparing for the birthday supper. It was as she had laid paper plates with pictures of balloons on them, along with paper cups, plastic knives and forks, and the rotting hedgehog cake that Krissi had demanded to know why she had done it, why she was doing this to them?

"The stuff, Krissi. I get it regular, get a roof over my head, get food. Don't have to suck cock or let stinking Pakis fuck me in the arse for a tenner a go... The stuff."

Her eyes were dead, and whenever she turned them from her tasks to look at Krissi directly, Krissi felt a cold worm turn in her heart. How could she have not seen what her old friend had become, a living dead thing kept alive only by the poison it put into itself?

She'd been recruited a year before. Mr Bartleby had come home and had found one of the old Skeleton Gang vulnerable, an addict so far gone that she would do anything for a fix of the *stuff*. Mr Bartleby wasn't a stranger to how drugs could be used to coerce people into doing awful things, and so he had used her as a puppet, and she in turn had manipulated the others by social media, spying on them, reporting what she saw, so that the lollipop man could dream up his sick revenge for their slighting him ten years before.

She had one last thing to tell Krissi before she stopped speaking to her, no matter how much Krissi cajoled or begged.

"He's the devil, Krissi. He's the devil."

"Then what he fuck does that make you?" Krissi had asked, her voice low and deathly cold.

This was when Adele had gagged Krissi by wrapping duct tape around her mouth. Krissi thrashed her head about trying to prevent it, but then Sam had moaned from across the table;

"Mummy, just let her. Please. Do what they want and they'll let us go."

And so she had relented.

When Mr Bartleby had come back down again his face was a mass of sticking plasters and bound gauze. He had also changed into a shirt and tie, and looked just like an ordinary man.

"I'll go and see a private doctor tomorrow and get myself fixed up properly. But tonight is all about you, Christine," he told her; though what had come out of his mouth was actually "Ah go an see a piyate dogor tomowwow an ged mysell fissed uh brobbablee..."

Krissi had felt a surge of savage glee when she saw him with his face patched together face, but this was smothered almost instantly when she saw Sam flinch as the lollipop man placed a hand on his shoulder.

She had jerked in her chair as if she could burst free and fall on him.

Mr Bartleby had grinned, wincing a little as he did so.

"Sho," he said. "Lesh ged dish pardee sdarded!"

*****

"We alwesh hed fish hun chebs fur birffdaa subba wen ah wesh liddle," said Mr Bartleby as he ladled out portions of battered fish and greasy, salty, vinegar soaked chips onto the paper plates sat in front of them. "A spesshel treed. An gaygg fur desserd!"

Adele pulled out a box cutting knife and slit the cable ties on Sam's right wrist.

Then she did the same for Krissi, never meeting her gaze.

As soon as her hand was free, Krissi was clawing at the duct tape that had kept her silent.

"You fucking bastard!" she cried at the lollipop man as soon as her lips could move. "Let him go! He's just a child!"

Mr Bartleby had already forked up a mouthful of tender white cod wrapped in crunchy batter, and he spoke with his mouth full, which made his response even more incomprehensible than before;

"Ahhn ferri addracdiff ee iss doo!"

Krissi's brain took a few seconds to puzzle out the meaning;

And very attractive he is too!

She lurched forward, swiping with her free hand, as far as she could reach with her other wrist still tied to the chair. She couldn't quite reach him, even as she leaned over so far the food in front of her was squashed under her breasts.

"Don't you fucking dare!" she screamed at him. "Don't you even think it, you fucking shit, I'll fucking kill you!"

He wagged a finger at her, and swallowed.

"Derrible dable madders! Eed jor subbah beffor id ged gold!"

Then he looked at Sammy.

"Add joo! Ef joo dobe eed jor subbah joo wond ged addy gayg!"

Krissi wanted to kill him every time he looked at, spoke too, touched her child. What had she been thinking when she had the gun and hadn't turned it on him, hadn't shot him over and over again in his hideous fucking face? But she could never have realised that her hatred had no bottom to it, was able to deepen, to thicken, when she saw Sam with tears crawling down his cheeks, pick up his plastic fork and start to eat the food in front of him.

If you don't eat your supper you won't get any cake!

Do what they want and they'll let us go.

She subsided, but her eyes never stopped staring at the lollipop man.

"I am going to kill you," she told him. Her voice was reasonable, even casual. She had simply stated a fact, a certainty, something that was inevitable; the sky was blue, the grass was green, she was going to kill this man.

Mr Bartleby stopped moving, a forkful of fish halfway to his mouth.

Krissi's face felt stiff, but she wasn't sure what set of her expression could have made that look of fear flash through the man's eyes.

All she knew was that no matter what happened, she was going to kill him.

"Eed jor foo," he told her quietly.

Krissi said nothing. She was aware that Sam was looking at her, but she mustn't allow herself to glance at him, because his face would break her heart and she couldn't let go of her fury, not now.

"Eed.Jor.Foo."

Her eyes never leaving his, Krissi picked up the paper party plate in front of her, lifted it, and tipped the whole lot onto the floor.

Mr Bartleby sat for a moment in total silence and stillness.

Then he sighed, put down his fork, and stood up.

"Fide.Joo wand jor gayg fust? Fide! Joo gan ab jor gayg fust!"

Fine. You want your cake first? Fine! You can have your cake first!

He grabbed at the rotting hedgehog cake in the middle of the table, his fingers clawing into the maggoty mass of melted, fungus furred chocolate sponge, until he picked up a packed snowball of the filthy stuff.

He plopped it on the table in front of Krissi.

"Eed id," he told her.

She stared at him.

"Eed id," he said again.

She said nothing. Her eyes said everything.

"Eed id," said Mr Bartleby. "Or ah will pud mah thub ub Sabby's arrs, ad den mayg jog lig de shid ob id."

...or I will put my thumb up Sammy's arse, and then make you lick the shit off it.

His eyes were flat, his ruined mouth set in a grim line.

He meant it.

She almost looked at Sam. Almost.

But instead, her gaze locked with the lollipop mans, she picked up the misshapen ball of decaying food and, like it was an apple, took a large bite.

Rot on her tongue, sour and sharp. Her stomach lurched. Her mouth flooded with saliva almost instantly, the glands in her jaw aching as they were pressed into sudden and furious action.

But worse was the texture. The fluff of the fungus was like candyfloss, gluing itself to the roof of her mouth. Her teeth slid through the juicy bodies of maggots buried in cake dough that was as sludgy as diarrhoea.

The taste and the texture combined were almost too much. If you'd told Krissi she was eating somebody's vomit, she could have believed it.

It was only the fire of her anger that allowed her to chew the rotten cake into a paste she could swallow, as the heat in her guts scorched away the worst of her nausea.

It felt like a huge slug had slimed its way down her throat, or she had swallowed the spunk of a dozen men all at once.

Mr Bartleby grinned.

"Goog! An now joo fad jor gayg, leds blay ah pardee gayb!"

And so saying he walked out of the room, rubbing his hands.

Krissi didn't look at her son.

She looked at Adele.

"If you have any soul left," she whispered quickly, pausing only to *urrp* as her a tide of nausea clenched her belly, "you'll cut us free, now, whilst he's gone."

The junkie was using her plastic fork to rake the same few chips back and forth on her plate.

"He killed our friends, and you helped him. And what do you think is going to happen to my son? If he's done all the stuff he says he's done, you know..." she drew a shuddering breath, not wanting to say it, not wanting Sam to hear or to speak the words because they may become real, "...you know it would be better if we were both dead. So, either cut us free and help us escape, or just cut our throats before that monster comes back. Better dead than that."

Adele looked up. Her dead eyes were suddenly sharp, brighter than at any time since Krissi had known her as a kid... like the child she had known was looking out at her, and Adele's ravaged face was only a mask of a future that may come, but didn't have to.

"You're right," she said softly. "I didn't... when you're hooked, that's it, you can't think about anything else but the next fix. Sometimes I thought about getting help, but my parents had already disowned me when he came along. He gave me as much as I wanted, whenever I wanted, and I never had to do the sick things anymore, the stuff blokes only come to a smackhead whore for because no-one else will do them. But he made me do other stuff, and... I think I died. I died with the twins, and then I died with Celina, and then Tony..."

Krissi felt her pulse quicken.

Adele had put down her fork and had produced the box cutting knife again. She slid three, four segments out.

"Yes," said Krissi.

But then Adele was smiling.

"It doesn't matter if I die one more time," said the little girl lost inside the withered woman, and plunged the knife into her throat.

Krissi gasped, wanting to scream but having nothing inside her.

She looked at Sam. His face was white and waxy looking and utterly unmoving. Shock. He'd gone into shock, and couldn't stop looking as Adele gripped the knife's handle with both hands and drew the blade through her throat, and at first it just looked like he was drawing an unsteady line with a bright red marker pen, until she got to the point where a man would have an Adam's apple and the blade seemed to stick. Grunting with the effort, she gave two hard jerks and cut through the hyoid bone, and where she had already sliced through opened like a lip-less mouth, an idiotic grin lacking teeth, full of blood that spilled out.

"Sam, puppy, look away, look away!"

But the child couldn't, not even as Adele finished opening her throat and, with a curious noise almost like a post-orgasm sigh, she placed the knife down beside her plate, then lay down in her food and died.

Mr Bartleby strolled back in, his lollipop man uniform draped over his arm, the lollipop itself in his free hand.

He did a small double take, frowning at the corpse lying face down in a mush of blood and battered fish. His eyes whipped from Krissi to Sam then back to Krissi again, confirming that they were both still secured.

"She killed herself," said Krissi in a very quiet, distant voice.

Mr Bartleby placed his uniform on the kitchen counter and leaned his lollipop against the fridge. He stepped around to Adele's side of the table, gripped her hair, and lifted her face out of her food. Chips, the small crispy ones you find at the bottom of a portion, clung to her face by their grease. Mr Bartleby shook her head and the chips fell off in a rain, along with a splatter of blood from her cut throat.

He stood there for a moment, thinking.

Krissi felt her gorge rising, looking at the slit throat that yawned wider and wider as the weight of Adele's body sagged downwards, causing the skin at either end of the cut to split, widening the wound.

"Puppy, please don't look?" she whispered.

But Sam was gone. His face was bloodless, and his eyes had come unfocused.

The lollipop man was roused from his thoughts by Krissi's words.

"Shayy, ah ford gwee gud do da pardee ganes oww, bud how aboud shum pubbedree furs?" he said.

Krissi was in too much shock to apply herself to translate her smashed and slurred speech, and more so when he picked up the box cutting knife and went to work at slicing through the rest of Adele's throat.

He worked like he was carving meat, fingers wrapped in her hair to keep her in place as the razor sharp knife slid back and forth, parting skin and fat and muscle. The sagging body helped, and in seconds Adele's head was only still connected to her body by the off-white knobbly looking thing in the back of her neck.

Her spine, and something slimy clinging to it, like squid flesh; her spinal column.

Mr Bartleby eased her body down lower in her seat until the exposed spine was level with the back of the chair.

He leaned her neck backwards, as for a moment Krissi pictured herself bending her client's heads back so that she could shampoo their hair before she got to work styling it.

Still holding Adele's hair, Mr Bartleby raised his elbow and brought it smashing down on the dead women's forehead.

The spine snapped. The hair slithered through his fingers and Adele's head hit the floor, leaving a ruined stump between her shoulders, oozing blood.

The lollipop man squatted down to pick up the head.

Whilst down there, he did something else.

He peeked over the table at his guests, grinning.

Adele's head popped up beside his.

"Ahhfurreeunnggee!" he said, trying not to move his lips, even as Adele's jaw flapped, only slightly in time with the words.

Sayyy, I thought we could do the party games now... but how about some puppetry first?

He'd jammed his hand up her ragged throat, shoving his fingers into her sinuses and under her soft pallet.

He smashed her face into her paper plate full of mashed up fish and chips and blood, and smeared it back and forth, making the jaws worked as if she were eating.

"OM NOMMM NOOMMMNNOMM!" he roared, before exploding into shrill, cracked laughter.

Krissi didn't even feel herself going. One moment she was watching the single most terrible thing she had ever seen in her life, and the next merciful blackness took her away from reality before madness could claim her.

FOURTEEN

"EBBEREE BUBBEES vavvoreed gayde, bin de dale on dee donggee!"

After he said this, Krissi's mind finally stopped hearing his broken toothed and lipless exclamations as nonsense that had to be translated. Her brain had enough information to offer her real time translations. She'd had a client two years ago who had had a huge stroke, and had found the entire left side of her body paralysed; this included her mouth, so that whenever she tried to speak she had sounded almost incoherently drunk. But over time, as Krissi had gotten so used to how she spoke, she no longer heard the speech impediment anymore.

It had taken some time for that mental software to kick in during the present nightmare, but now it had.

She wished to God it had not.

Mr Bartleby raised an eyebrow.

"There's nothing like a little enthusiasm..." he said, his words still mushy *–nuffen lahg a liddle annfushiashim-* but there was no delay between his meaning and her understanding, "...and that was nothing like a little enthusiasm! This is everybody's favourite game, pin the tail on the donkey!"

A box cutting knife. A gun.

Either would have done.

Even her bare hands.

Her teeth.

Her hands were bound, as were her legs, and her mouth was once more sealed with duct tape. She was naked and the floor was cold and gritty.

She could not move or cry out. In the first minutes after she had regained consciousness and seen what was on the floor, and who was stood so close by, she had been a frenzied, rabid animal. Krissi was familiar with the belief that a parent could find themselves in possession of enormous strength when a child was in danger, to the point where they could lift a crashed car to rescue their baby, but if it were true she was not so blessed. Despite her thrashing and straining, the cable ties did not break, but only cut deeply into her flesh to the point where she was bleeding.

Mr Bartleby had watched with a fascinated expression on his ruined face.

Then he had hauled her to her feet.

"Even though I'm rich as fuck, the things I need are fairly cheap," he said. "Cable ties, tape... I've had a lot of practice, can you tell?"

He was a lot stronger than he looked, helping Krissi up without even a grunt of exertion. She tottered; the cable ties were bound around her knees as they had been on Nadia, leaving her able to stand and even to shuffle-walk, but very unsteadily.

She cried out when he ripped the duct tape from her mouth, but the brief pain was nothing compared to her overriding instinct to go to her child. She tried to get to Sam, but the lollipop man pulled her back, and then stood in front of her as a barrier.

Krissi didn't charge him. She had been trying to avoid looking at him.

He was naked.

Almost naked.

The man was naked save for his hi-vis trench-coat, which was unbuttoned to show a sunken chest, a pot belly, and something enormous and evil looking hanging between his scrawny thighs.

When she had seen it, she had wondered what the hell it was, then when the answer was almost articulated in her mind she had discarded the thought. It was only recognisable as male anatomy from the general shape, and the fact that it was between his legs.

He explained.

"They weren't always virgins when I got 'em," he said. "Actually, a lot of them were broken in pretty well... me and the other bad blokes would trade our favourites around, and suffice to say, a lot of 'emwere fairly filthy when I dipped my wick. My old chap is a living encyclopaedia of STIs... Except for crabs, of course, because they need pubes to live in..."

Half of its size must have been from swelling induced by infection, that and massive injury; it was bruised looking, mottled with disturbing shades of purple and blue and black, its end thicker than the root as if it were pendulous with pus. The length of the thing was studded with cancerous looking warts, including a cluster on the very end of the foreskin. They had whitish growths like antlers, making Krissi think of the eyes of a potato left too long in the back of a cupboard.

Maybe her distress and disgust excited him, as the thing twitched and began to swell.

Or maybe it was Sam, naked on the floor.

The lollipop man gripped himself with his free hand and began to work his decaying inches. In response it firmed and rose skyward, lengthening, thickening, and displaying an underbelly that was a mottled with yellow eyed boils that swarmed across his scrotum and all the way up the shaft like diseased barnacles on the hull of a rotting boat. He gave himself a long, hard squeeze, and a couple of the smaller ones burst, sending miniature ejaculations of bloody pus over his knuckles.

"You'd think with all my dosh I'd have bought myself a clean bill of health, but the truth is, I like the stinging and the relentless itch..."

So saying, he clawed at his scrotum. Flakes of dead skin, huge snowflakes of dandruff, burst like blossom from the withered and hairless sack.

"Like sweet and sour, pleasure needs to be balanced out with a little pain..."

Krissi vomited. Stringy bile flowed over her lips and fell onto her own feet, a bile mixed with maggots and churned up, fungus riddled cake flesh.

Mr Bartleby laughed.

"Probably best you didn't finish your supper! Alright then, let's play pin the tail on the donkey!" He wagged the diseased thing between his thighs at her. "I'm ready, how about you?"

"Sam?" Krissi croaked, ignoring the madman. "Puppy, are you okay?"

It was a weak, pathetic thing to say, but it was all she could think to do, to ask that most basic and fundamental question, the question people ask even in the event of a car crash or a bomb blast.

He was curled into a fetal position on the floor. Naked.

He said nothing. His eyes were open, but there was no sign of Sam in them.

"Puppy?" she whispered.

Nothing. His face betrayed no emotion or understanding, and the only sign that he was even alive was the rise and fall of his thin chest, and the occasional slow blink of his eyelids.

Sam was gone.

For a heartbeat of a moment, a thought darted through her mind which she was ashamed of... a hope, a wish, barely articulated... that Sam would never come back. He'd seen too much, heard too much.

And worse was coming.

"The game is simple, dearest Christine," said Mr Bartleby. "First one to pin the tail on the donkey wins! Got it? You look a bit blank. Okay, let me put it in laymen's terms; the first one of us to get our cock up your son's arse wins. But don't worry that you don't have one, I've got you sorted!"

Mr Bartleby waved the lollipop back and forth, then lifted it up and turned it upside down.

The thin end had been modified. He had jammed a dildo onto it, a hard black silicone thing at least a foot long and as thick as a beer can.

"You're completely fucking insane," said Krissi. She said it quietly, with awe in her voice, learning a truth that she could never have conceived about the world; that there existed a depth of evil so far beyond the experience of the average human being, that it could only be known by the name of insanity.

Having given himself over to the endless exploration and indulgence of every wicked thought he ever had, Mr Bartleby had passed beyond humanity.

He walked behind Krissi, keeping the gun trained on her so that she didn't move.

"Just picture yourself as a witch, riding a broomstick!" he told her, standing behind her, and jammed the business end of the lollipop between her thighs so that the sex toy end was sticking out from her clenched crotch.

Then everything went black. Something was slipped over her head, over her eyes, and was fastened quickly around the back of her skull.

It was sticky.

"Got to be blindfolded, it ain't pin the tail on the donkey if you can see! Don't worry, I'm putting one on as well, though mine ain't soaked with superglue... there! Blind as a fucking bat that's had its eye gouged out!"

The blackness was almost complete. The material of whatever he had blindfolded her with allowed just enough light through to see blurred and shadowy outlines against the greater mass of shadows beyond them. Her skin tingled across her brow and under her eyes; superglue, bonding with her skin She kept her thighs clenched, the pole held between them just like a witch on a broomstick like he had said, the obscene thing jutting out ahead of her.

Then she was being spun around and around, only just keeping her balance. He had gripped her hands and swung her around and around, as if they were dancing a mad jig

"Wheeeeeee!" said Mr Bartleby.

He let go and she tottered backwards, feeling herself about to fall until her shoulder crashed into the wall, a sudden flare of pain.

She heard blundering footsteps to her left as the blindfolded lollipop man also tried to keep his balance.

"I won't cheat!" called Mr Bartleby. "It wouldn't be any fun that way! I told you the rules, didn't I? Whoever fucks Sam first, wins!"

He swore.

"Cunt, just smacked the wall! Ooh, that stings!"

"What do I get if I win?"

Krissi was surprised to hear herself speak. Some impulse of her subconscious had prompted the question that her conscious mind at first failed to grasp the implications of. She was still where she had ended up, leaning on the wall.

"Win? What do you think Christine, you win your freedom! I'll let you both go and I'll fuck off out of your lives forever, head back East and build up a new stable..."

"And what if you win?"

She refused to acknowledge what winning would mean. She just wanted to know the terms.

She wasn't going to... no.

Never.

"Well, if I win, the first thing I'll do is slice off your eyelids so you have to watch everything I do afterwards."

Krissi stood up straight, gently shoving herself away from the wall.

What was she doing?

She took small, shuffling steps forward, which were all her cable tied knees would allow, still clenching the thin shaft of the lollipop between her thighs. She turned slightly to her left, and felt the round sign of the lollipop scrape against the wall. She moved further away so that she could turn fully, facing what she felt was the centre of the room.

What was she doing?

Sam had been lying on the ground more or less in the middle of the room.

She reached up and tugged at the blindfold. It was bonded to her skin; when she tried to pull it away, she might as well have been trying to pull the flesh from around her eyes.

Over to her right, she heard Mr Bartleby's feet thudding the floor, his hands slapping the wall. He was giggling softly. Through her blindfold, a patch of deeper darkness was crawling across the lighter darkness. Looking down, all was shadows.

The sign end of the lollipop was heavier than the thin end, where the dildo jutted forward out of her crotch. The see-saw effect meant she felt it sticking up at an acute angle in front of her, just like a real erection.

She wasn't doing this.

She wasn't thinking it.

She moved slowly, not only because the tied cutting into the backs of her knees forced her to take tiny steps, but because she didn't want to be heard.

Heard by who?

By Mr Bartleby. She couldn't alert him that...

Say it.

He wouldn't believe that she was going to...

Say it.

That was why he was mucking about, pretending to be lost, slapping the wall in exaggeration. He thought he had plenty of time because Krissi would never contemplate...

SAY IT.

It was better she did it than him.

She reached down with her bound wrists and her fingers found the thing sticking out in front of her.

It was enormous, the size of a horse, but cold and dry.

No.

No.

She was going to get to Sam, get him up on his feet, and they were going to get away.

That wasn't going to happen. There was only one way out of here.

Yes. There was only one way.

*****

He hadn't an original thought in his head, not really. The game they were playing wasn't his invention. He'd played it before, been introduced to it by one of his friends, a remarkable Australian who controlled a significant proportion of the flow of heroin out of the golden triangle. They'd played it with a number of other members of the Club one long, glorious weekend in Pattaya. The Australian was a great believer in giving back to the villages where the opium poppy was grown, and had built many schools along the northern border... including schools for those orphaned by the anti-drug government skirmishes in the area, and for physically and mentally disabled children, who were traditionally abandoned by the Hmong tribes people who called the jungle home.

Abandoned, orphaned, wouldn't be missed.

Mr Bartleby could barely stop himself from ripping off his blindfold to see what the Skelton girl was doing. Probably pissing herself in a corner of the room, having gone into shock, like the boy had.

It was a shame.

He hated when they drifted away like that, their souls abandoning their bodies either just before or during. It took a certain amount of the edge off proceedings when you couldn't see the pain and terror, hear their screams and sobs... and all that delicious slobber that accumulated on their faces, that special mixture of snot and tears that collected on their lips and chin to be licked off…

No, he would keep his blindfold on, play the game properly, even if he knew she was never going to join in.

He pushed himself away from the wall, aiming for the middle of the room. He was still dizzy from the spinning, and his footsteps were as unsteady as a drunk. He held one hand out in front of him, sweeping the air slowly so that he wouldn't crash into another wall if he missed the boy and ended up crossing the room, with his other hand slowly squeezing and rubbing his diseased cock.

Something jabbed him in the hip.

It was involuntary; he said, "Ow."

And the Skelton girl said;

"Found you."

*****

The dildo had probed the blundering dark and then encountered something solid. She'd been using it as a guide, swaying her hips back and forth like visually impaired people did with their white canes, feeling her way forward.

The dark said "Ow."

"Found you."

She hadn't meant to speak, it had just come out.

Her bound hands shot up, blundering across his chest until she found his throat.

But with her wrists bound, effectively turning her hands into a butterfly, she wasn't able to secure a grip around his neck.

"Get off me, bitch!"

He shoved her away.

She tottered backwards, almost keeping her balance.

She tripped over Sam.

She sprawled backwards, falling in a confused tangle that bent the shaft of the lollipop as she hit the gritty, cold floorboards on the other side of Sam's prone body. There was pain and confusion, but the second she had her wits about her, her first thought was of her son.

"Sam puppy, are you okay? Sam, please, are you alright? Sam? Sam?"

She thrashed on the ground, her bound limbs and the bent pole between her legs making her unable to flip herself over.

"Oh, you've found him!" said Mr Bartleby. "Keep chatting Christine, guide me to you!"

His footsteps were suddenly the loudest thing in the world.

The lollipop man was coming for her, for Sam.

Krissi screamed, needing to see the threat she reached up and dug her nails into the blindfold and began to rip at it, her nails clawing at the fabric until they dug in and she pulled as hard as she could.

She could only drag it down as it was still tied at the back of her head, but even so, the pain was incredible as she ripped away her own skin along with the blindfold, long strips peeling away like rotting wallpaper, creating a domino mask of raw flesh around her eyes. It felt like someone had drawn spectacles on her face in lighter fluid, and then set it on fire.

She could see again, watering eyes glaring out of the ruin of her face as she pulled the shredded blindfold and skin down under her chin.

Still wearing his own blindfold, grinning with his mouth full of impossibly white teeth and his hands raised and clutching, Mr Bartleby was stumbling towards her and Sam.

The child hadn't reacted to her falling backwards over him. His eyes were still open and still blank. Catatonic.

The shaft of the lollipop had bent under her, but the dildo still pointed up proudly.

Mr Bartleby was moving more slowly, sweeping his foot in front of him, looking for Sam.

That was all she could stand.

Krissi knew what she had to do.

She scooted forward as much as she could, wriggling her back and hips to get as far from Sam as she could.

"Come and get him you twisted peedo fuck!" she screamed.

The foot stopped sweeping and the grin grew wider.

"Gotcha!" said Mr Bartleby.

He stumbled forward. Towards her.

Krissi drew her legs up as far as she could, and when he was looming over her and Sam she kicked as hard as she could at his shins.

His forward momentum, coupled with the sudden shunt to his legs, caused him to fall forward with a croaking cry of disbelief.

Krissi arched her back, thrusting her crotch up, her thighs clenched, holding the bent lollipop pole upright.

The lollipop man fell on the tip of the dildo.

It punched into his pasty potbelly, just below his navel; with the bent end of the stick braced against the floorboards under Krissi's legs, he might as well have been falling onto a spear.

Twelve inches of solid latex slid up into him, burrowing through his intestines, shoving his internal organs apart and ripping through arteries, the tip suddenly popping through his back, just to the right of his spine, slightly below his ribs.

His face hung above hers. His eyes were still covered by the blindfold, but his mouth formed a perfectly round O of surprise.

Krissi reached up and pulled the blindfold down.

His eyes were also round, lacking comprehension. He had no idea what had just happened.

His body slid down further until he was nose to nose with Krissi, the end of the dildo that stuck through his back causing his hi-vis trench-coat to tent.

He tried to say something, and belched a bloody burp into her face instead.

"I had a boyfriend once," Krissi told him, her voice casual but quiet, eyes glaring like furnaces in their raw and bloody craters, "who had a weird way of referring to fucking. He used to say, 'I'm gonna get up to my nuts in guts.' Don't think he meant this though."

Her hands were splayed out straight above her head. She brought them up and over the back of his head, almost like she was clasping a lover. When her bound wrists were locked tight behind his neck, that was when she started to rut, thrusting her fake cock up into him as deeply as she could, fucking the wound wider, feeling blood raining onto her bare belly, and when he was open enough, the warm coils of his guts dropped onto her.

She didn't stop until she felt his heartbeat flutter and fade.

FIFTEEN

SHE SAW the lollipop man before Sam did, and froze.

How could they?

Everyone knew what they had been through only a year ago, and even if they had no idea about the seemingly endless therapy sessions and the nights when Sam woke up screaming every hour, surely they had more common sense, more decency than to actually go ahead...

But a little girl had been run down two months before, and many parents had pointed to the fact that they all knew it was inevitable; who hadn't heard of some child who had had a near-miss on that busy main road? There had been a meeting of the PTA, and information delivered to all nearby concerned groups, and yes, what had happened to the Skelton's -the bare bones at least; the press were never allowed to reveal the true extant of it, yet still it had been headline news- was spoken about, but the possible trauma that the boy might, might, experience was nothing compared to a repeat of the tragedy of a little girl who would not be coming home again... Her hand went up to the domino mask of scar tissue around her eyes where she had ripped her on skin off, the shiny patchwork of grafted flesh a constant reminder that the nightmare had been real.

So engrossed with her train of thought was Krissi that it was Sam who had to rouse her, gently tugging her hand with his.

"It's okay mummy," he said. "I'm not scared. The bad one is dead."

He'd seen the bright yellow figure leading children across the road, and his fear was inexpertly hidden behind a forced smile.

He was trying so hard.

He was talking more than he used to, thanks to the therapy.

But he didn't draw anymore, and his eyes were older than they should have been.

The therapist had told her that children could recover from horrific events that would make adults need to take medication for the rest of their lives, and this was apparently true; Sam was still Sam, even with those older eyes, but she hadn't slept a night without a pill since it happened.

"We can cross elsewhere..."

"It's okay mummy."

"Are you sure puppy?"

He nodded.

They were part of a stream of parents and their children and the occasional dog being multi-tasked into the morning commute. The weather was chilly but clear and dry. The stream moved faster than them, it seemed, for when they reached the point in the road that was patrolled, they found themselves there alone, the lollipop man on the other pavement waving good bye and good morning to the last knot he had helped across the road.

He looked back, across the road at them.

It was him.

For one second, it was him.

But it wasn't, of course. It never would be.

A voice from years ago sounded lost and far in her memory; *peeee-doooo...*

Sam's hand clutched hers.

The lollipop man was an older man with a leathery face and a lot of laughter lines around his kind blue eyes. He raised his lollipop and advanced into the road, halting the traffic.

When he reached their side he was smiling.

"Well, good morning young man! A pleasure to make your acquaintance!"

Sam smiled shyly.

"You're Australian," said Krissi.

The lollipop man hunkered down to look at Sam on the boy's level. He didn't look at her at all, even as he replied.

"That I surely am, ma'am. Name's Blue... and you must be Samuel, right? Well, you'd best get used to this ugly mug, because you're going to be seeing an awful lot of me!"

AUTHOR'S NOTE

PART OF my day job involved going to collect the company's post each morning, which is nice as I get to spend an hour or so out and about listening to the radio, flipping between Planet Rock and SAM FM. My route used to take me along a main road outside a primary school, and being first thing in the morning this meant that I was driving down it during the school run, both pavements filled with excitable kids, often on scooters, being pursued by parents trying to walk the family dog at the same time. For the longest time my journey would always be interrupted by the lollipop man spotting me and stepping into the traffic flow to create safe passage for the children on their way to their lessons; the company vehicle I drive is huge and emblazoned with the firm's logo, and I guess he picked me as one of those vehicles he knew he could safely halt because, A) he knew from experience I'm a careful and considerate driver, and B) driving a vehicle with the company's name splattered all over it meant I'd never dare act the cunt.

Then one morning he wasn't there.

I didn't think much of it. But then he wasn't there the next morning, or the next, or the rest of that week.

Well, everyone goes on holiday, right? He'd be back after a week or two.

But he never did come back.

After that, the parents had to arrange their own method of safely getting their spawn across the road, which was basically a group of them collecting along one part of the pavement until critical mass was reached, forcing one of them to make a dash for it, dragging the dog and kid across by their throats and wrists respectively; this then resulted in a lemming like flood of big and little people, which would halt my progress because, well, see points A and B above.

To be honest, about a month after the lollipop man vanished I changed my route. I am a careful driver, and not just because the company vehicle would make it easy to track me down if I decided to drive like a cunt; weirdly enough, for a person who writes extreme horror, I actually have no desire to mow down a bunch of scab-kneed and pigtailed brats skipping to school.

I did idly wonder why the lollipop man vanished. I mean, I knew the reason had to be budget cuts, but the imp which is my muse wondered if maybe there wasn't another reason for the fluorescent guardian of the tarmac to have upped and fucked off… At some point, working away down there in the subconscious place that stories come from, the imp began to speculate if a lollipop man wouldn't make a deliciously silly sort of home-grown slasher icon, a supernatural serial killer that was as British as jingoism or crisp sandwiches or swans that can break your arm, in a field largely dominated by American made maniacs like Mr Voorhess and Mr Kreuger.

For me, the act of storytelling is a lot like those parents trying to cross the road with their kids. There's a build-up of ideas, and then when it gets to critical mass there's a sudden flood, and I find myself writing

It was a lot of fun thinking up ways for Mr Bartleby to dispatch the kids who'd pissed him off, and I was grinning like a wanking chimp all the way through the process of getting the words down… until the final third when things took that unbelievably dark turn.

I don't go in for romanticising writing. Fundamentally, it's a weird thing to do, to plop your arse in a seat and spend hours making stuff up. But one thing any writer will tell you is, sometimes, the fucking story leaves your control. And that happened here; I did not mean to write anything so dark, but somehow that sick fuck Bartleby got away from me and my silly slasher mutated into a bleak look at one of the most grotesque realities of our world.

Men like him exist. The things they do are real.

Somewhere on this planet right now, what they do is happening.

And sometimes I wonder, what's the point of plopping my arse in a seat and making up horrors, when the world is already choking on them?

Oh dear.

Things got a bit dark in the final third of this afterword, didn't they?

Kevin Sweeney

www.ingramcontent.com/pod-product-compliance
Lightning Source LLC
Chambersburg PA
CBHW071917220626
47052CB00002B/388
9781838461300